WEATHER REPORT FROM
THE TWILIGHT ZONE

TEMPERATURE:
uncanny, bone-chilling cold.

VISIBILITY:
unlimited to the farthest reaches of infinity.

WINDS:
fresh breezes of eerie madness increased to the point of
sheer unbearableness.

FORECAST:
delirious, heartstopping pleasure for every connoisseur
of the strange, the wonderful, and the unexpected.

STORIES FROM
THE TWILIGHT ZONE

STORIES FROM THE TWILIGHT ZONE

BY ROD SERLING

RLI: $\dfrac{\text{VLM } 6.0}{\text{IL } 7\text{–}12}$

STORIES FROM THE TWILIGHT ZONE
A Bantam Book / April 1960

2nd printing ...... April 1960	8th printing .... March 1961
3rd printing ...... April 1960	9th printing ...... May 1961
4th printing ...... June 1960	10th printing ... October 1961
5th printing .... August 1960	11th printing .... April 1962
6th printing .... October 1960	12th printing .... August 1962
7th printing .. November 1960	13th printing .... March 1963

Bantam Pathfinder edition / December 1964

15th printing . December 1964	21st printing .... March 1969
16th printing . September 1965	22nd printing ..... April 1971
17th printing ..... June 1966	23rd printing . September 1971
18th printing . December 1966	24th printing .... March 1972
19th printing ... October 1967	25th printing ... October 1972
20th printing ... January 1969	26th printing ... August 1973

27th printing .. November 1974
Bantam edition / December 1975
29th printing

Library of Congress Catalog Card Number: 64-7966

Published simultaneously in the United States and Canada

Bantam Books are published by Bantam Books, Inc. Its trade-
mark, consisting of the words "Bantam Books" and the por-
trayal of a bantam, is registered in the United States Patent
Office and in other countries. Marca Registrada. Bantam
Books, Inc., 666 Fifth Avenue, New York, New York 10019.

PRINTED IN THE UNITED STATES OF AMERICA

Table of Contents

For my brother Bob,
the first writer of the Serling clan

The Mighty Casey

There is a large, extremely decrepit stadium over-grown by weeds and high grass that is called, whenever it is referred to (which is seldom nowadays), Tebbet's Field and it lies in a borough of New York known as Brooklyn. Many years ago it was a baseball stadium housing a ball club known as the Brooklyn Dodgers, a major league baseball team then a part of the National League. Tebbet's Field today, as we've already mentioned, houses nothing but memories, a few ghosts and tier after tier of decaying wooden seats and cracked concrete floors. In its vast, gaunt emptiness nothing stirs except the high grass of what once was an infield and an outfield, in addition to a wind that whistles through the screen behind home plate and howls up to the rafters of the overhang of the grandstand.

This was one helluva place in its day, and in its day, the Brooklyn Dodgers was one rip-roaring ball club. In the last several years of its existence, however, it was referred to by most of the ticket-buying, turnstile-passers of Flatbush Avenue as "the shlumpfs!". This arose from the fact that for five years running, the Brooklyn Dodgers were something less than spectacular. In their last year as members of the National League, they won exactly forty-nine ball games. And by mid-August of that campaign a "crowd" at Tebbet's Field was considered to be any ticket-buying group of more than eighty-six customers.

After the campaign of that year, the team dropped out of the league. It was an unlamented, unheralded event pointing up the fact that baseball fans have a penchant for winners and a short memory for losers. The paying customers proved more willing to travel uptown to the Polo Grounds to see the Giants, or crosstown to Yankee Stadium to see the Yankees, or downtown to any movie theater or bowling alley than to watch the Brooklyn Dodgers stumble around in the basement of the league season after season. This is also commentative on the forgetfulness of baseball enthusiasts, since there are probably only a handful who recollect that for a wondrous month and a half, the Brooklyn Dodgers were a most unusual ball club that last season. They didn't start out as an unusual ball club. They started out as shlumpfs as any Dodger fan can articulately and colorfully tell you. But for one month and one half they were one helluva club. Principally because of a certain person on the team roster.

It all began this way. Once upon a time a most unusual event happened on the way over to the ball park. This unusual event was a left-hander named Casey!

It was try-out day for the Brooklyn Dodgers and Mouth McGarry, the manager of the club, stood in the dugout, one foot on the parapet, both hands shoved deep into his hip pockets, his jaw hanging several inches below his upper lip. "Try-out days" depressed Mouth Mc-Garry more than the standing of his ball club, which was depressing enough as it stood, or lay—which would be more apt, since they were now in last place, just thirty-one games out of first. Behind him, sitting on a bench, was Bertram Beasley, the general manager of the ball club. Beasley was a little man whose face looked like an X ray of an ulcer. His eyes were sunk deep into his little head, and his little head was sunk deep in between two narrow shoulder blades. Each time he looked up to survey Mc-Garry, and beyond him, several gentlemen in baseball uniforms, he heaved a deep sigh and saw to it that his head sank just a few inches deeper into his shoulder blades. The sigh Bertram Beasley heaved was the only respectable heave going on within a radius of three hundred feet of home plate. The three pitchers that scout Maxwell Jenkins had sent over turned out to be pitchers in name only. One of them, as a matter of fact, had looked so familiar that McGarry swore he'd seen him pitch in the 1911 World Series. As it turned out, McGarry had been mistaken. It was not he who had pitched in the 1911 World Series but his nephew.

Out on the field McGarry watched the current crop of try-outs and kept massaging his heart. Reading left to right they were a tall, skinny kid with three-inch-thick glasses; a seventeen-year-old fat boy who weighed about two hundred and eighty pounds and stood five-foot-two; a giant, hulking farm boy who had taken off his spike shoes; and the aforementioned "pitcher" who obviously had dyed his hair black, but it was not a fast color and the hot summer sun was sending black liquid down both sides of his face. The four men were in the process of doing calisthenics. They were all out of step except the aging pitcher who was no longer doing calisthenics. He had simply sat down and was fanning himself with his mitt.

Beasley rose from the bench in the dugout and walked over to McGarry. Mouth turned to look at him.

"Grand-looking boys!"

"Who were you expecting?" Beasley said, sticking a cigar in his mouth. "The All Stars? You stick out a try-out sign for a last division club—" he pointed to the group doing the calisthenics, "and this is the material you usually round up." He felt a surge of anger as he stared into the broken-nosed face of Mouth McGarry. "Maybe if you were any kind of a manager, McGarry, you'd be able to whip stuff like this into shape."

McGarry stared at him like a scientist looking through a microscope at a bug. "I couldn't whip stuff like that into shape," he said, "if they were eggs and I was an electric mixer. You're the general manager of the club. Why don't you give me some ballplayers?"

"You'd know what to do with them?" Beasley asked.

"Twenty games out of fourth place and the only big average we've got is a manager with the widest mouth in either league. Maybe you'd better get reminded that when the Brooklyn Dodgers win one game we gotta call it a streak! Buddy boy," he said menacingly, "when contract time comes around, *you* don't have to." His cigar went out and he took out a match and lit it. Then he looked up toward home plate where a pitcher was warming up. "How's Fletcher doing?" he asked.

"Are you kidding?" Mouth spat thirty-seven feet off to the left. "Last week he pitched four innings and allowed only six runs. That makes him our most valuable player of the month!"

The dugout phone rang and Beasley went over to pick it up. "Dugout," he said into the receiver. "What? Who?" He cupped his hand over the phone and looked over at Mouth. "You wanta look at a pitcher?" he asked.

"Are you kidding?" Mouth answered.

Beasley talked back into the phone. "Send him down," he said. He hung up the receiver and walked back over to Mouth. "He's a lefty," he announced.

"Lefty Shmefty," Mouth said. "If he's got more than one arm and less than four—he's for us!" He cupped his hands over his mouth and yelled out toward the field. "Hey, Monk!"

The catcher behind home plate rose from his squat and looked back over toward the dugout. "Yeah?"

"Fletcher can quit now," Mouth called to him. "I've got a new boy coming down. Catch him for a while."

"Check," the catcher said. Then he turned toward the pitcher. "Okay, Fletch. Go shower up."

Beasley walked back over to sit on the bench in the dugout. "You got the line-up for tonight?" he asked the manager.

"Working on it," Mouth said.

"Who starts?"

"You mean pitcher? I just feel them one by one. Whoever's warm goes to the mound." He spat again and put his foot back up on the parapet, staring out at the field. Once again he yelled out toward his ballplayers. "Chavez, stop already with the calisthenics."

He watched disgustedly as the three men stopped jumping up and down and the old man sitting on the ground looked relieved. Chavez thumbed them off the field and turned back toward the bench and shrugged a what-the-hell-can-I-do-with-things-like-this kind of shrug.

Mouth took out a handkerchief and wiped his face. He walked up the steps of the dugout and saw the sign sticking in the ground which read: "Brooklyn Dodgers —try-outs today." He pulled back his right foot and followed through with a vicious kick which sent the sign skittering along the ground. Then he went over to the third-base line, picked up a piece of grass and chewed it thoughtfully. Beasley left the dugout to join McGarry. He kneeled down alongside of him and picked up another piece of grass and began to chew. They knelt and lunched together until McGarry spit out his piece of grass and glared at Beasley.

"You know something, Beasley?" he inquired. "We are so deep in the cellar that our roster now includes an infield, an outfield and a furnace! And you know whose fault that is?"

Beasley spit out his own piece of grass and said, "You tell me!"

"It ain't mine," McGarry said defensively. "It just happens to be my luck to wind up with a baseball organization whose farm system consists of two silos and a McCormick reaper. The only thing I get sent up to me each spring is a wheat crop."

"McGarry," Beasley stated definitely, "if you had material, would you really know what to do with it? You ain't no Joe McCarthy. You ain't one half Joe McCarthy."

"Go die, will you," McGarry said. He turned back to stare down the third-base line at nothing in particular. He was unaware of the cherubic little white-haired man who had just entered the dugout. Beasley *did* see him and stared wide-eyed. The little old man came up behind Mouth and cleared his throat.

"Mr. McGarry?" he said. "I am Dr. Stillman. I called about your trying out a pitcher."

Mouth turned slowly to look at him, screwed up his

face in distaste. "All right! What's the gag? What about it, Grampa? Did this muttonhead put you up to it?" He turned to Beasley. "This is the pitcher, huh? Big joke. Yok, yok, yok. Big joke."

Dr. Stillman smiled benignly. "Oh, I'm not a pitcher," he said, "though I've thrown baseballs in my time. Of course, that was before the war."

"Yeah," Mouth interjected. "Which war? The Civil War? You don't look old enough to have spent the winter at Valley Forge." Then he glared at him intently. "Come to think of it—was it really as cold as they say?"

Stillman laughed gently. "You really have a sense of humor, Mr. McGarry." Then he turned and pointed toward the dugout. "Here's Casey now," he said.

Mouth turned to look expectantly over the little old man's shoulder. Casey was coming out of the dugout. From cleats to the button on top of his makeshift baseball cap there was a frame roughly six feet, six inches high. The hands at his sides were the dimensions of two good-sized cantaloupes. His shoulders, McGarry thought to himself, made Primo Carnero look like the "before" in a Charles Atlas ad. In short, Casey was long. He was also broad. And in addition, he was one of the most powerful men either McGarry or Beasley had ever seen. He carried himself with the kind of agile grace that bespeaks an athlete and the only jarring note in the whole picture was a face that should have been handsome, but wasn't, simply because it had no spark, no emotion, no expression of any sort at all. It was just a face. Nice teeth, thin lips, good straight nose, deep-set blue eyes, a shock of sandy hair that hung out from under his baseball cap. But it was a face, McGarry thought, that looked as if it had been painted on.

"You're the lefty, huh?" McGarry said. "All right." He pointed toward the home plate. "You see that guy with the great big mitt on? He's what's known as a catcher. His name is Monk. Throw a few into him."

"Thanks very much, Mr. McGarry," Casey said dully.

He went toward home plate. Even the voice, McGarry thought. Even the voice. Dead. Spiritless. McGarry picked up another long piece of grass and headed back to the dugout, followed by Beasley and the little old man who looked like something out of Charles Dickens. In the dugout, McGarry assumed his familiar pose of one foot on the parapet, both fists in his hip pockets. Beasley left the dugout to return to his office which was his custom on days the team didn't play. He would lock himself in his room and add up attendance figures, then look through the want ads of *The New York Times*. Just Stillman and Mouth McGarry stood in the dugout now, and the elderly little man watched everything with wide, fluttering eyes like a kid on a tour through a fireworks factory. McGarry turned to him.

"You his father?"

"Casey's?" Stillman asked. "Oh, no. He has no father. I guess you'd call me his—well, kind of his creator."

Dr. Stillman's words went past McGarry the way the super-chief goes by a water tank. "That a fact?" he asked rhetorically. "How old is he?"

"How old is he?" Stillman repeated. He thought for a moment. "Well, that's a little difficult to say."

Mouth looked over toward the empty bench with a see-the-kind-of-idiocy-I-have-to-put-up-with kind of look. "That's a little difficult to say," he mimicked fiercely.

Stillman hurriedly tried to explain. "What I mean is," he said, "it's hard to be chronological when discussing Casey's age. Because he's only been in existence for three weeks. What I mean is—he has the physique and mind of roughly a twenty-two-year-old, but in terms of how long he's been here—the answer to that would be about three weeks."

The words had poured out of Dr. Stillman's mouth and McGarry had blinked through the whole speech.

"Would you mind going over that again?" he asked.

"Not at all," Dr. Stillman said kindly. "It's really not too difficult. You see I made Casey. I built him." He smiled a big, beatific smile. "Casey's a robot," he said. The old man took a folded and creased document from his vest pocket and held it out to Mouth. "These are the blueprints I worked from," he said.

Mouth swatted the papers out of the old man's hand and dug his gnarled knuckles into the sides of his head.

That goddamn Beasley. There were no depths to which that sonofabitch wouldn't go to make his life miserable. He had to gulp several times before he could bring himself to speak to the old man and when finally words came, the voice didn't sound like his at all.

"Old friend," his voice came out in a wheeze. "Kind, sweet old man. Gentle grandfather, with the kind eyes, I am very happy that he's a robot. Of course, that's what he is." He patted Stillman's cheek. "That's just what he is, a nice robot." Then there was a sob in his voice as he glared up at the roof of the dugout. "Beasley, you crummy sonofabitch!" A robot yet. This fruity old man and that miserable ball club and the world all tumbling down and it just never ended and it never got any better. A robot!

Dr. Stillman scurried after Mouth who had walked up the steps of the dugout and out on to the field. He paused along the third-base line and began to chew grass again. Over his shoulder Casey was throwing pitches into the catcher at home plate, but Mouth didn't even notice him.

"I dunno," he said to nobody in particular. "I don't even know what I'm *doing* in baseball."

He looked uninterested as Casey threw a curve ball that broke sharply just a foot out in front of home plate and then shrieked into the catcher's mitt like a small, circular, white express train.

"That Beasley," Mouth said to the ground. "That guy's got as much right in the front office as I've got in the Alabama State Senate. This guy is a nothing, that's all. Simply a nothing. He was born a nothing. He's a nothing now!"

On the mound Casey wound up again and threw a hook that screamed in toward home plate, swerved briefly to the left, shot back to the right, and then landed in the catcher's mitt exactly where it had been placed as a target. Monk stared at the ball wide-eyed and then toward the young pitcher on the mound. He examined the ball, shook his head, then threw it back to him, shaking his head slowly from side to side.

Meanwhile Mouth continued his daily analysis of the

situation to a smiling Dr. Stillman and an empty grandstand. "I've had bum teams before," he was saying. "Real bad outfits. But this one!" He spat out the piece of grass. "These guys make Abner Doubleday a criminal! You know where I got my last pitcher? He was mowing the infield and I discovered that he was the only guy on the club who could reach home plate from the pitcher's mound on less than two bounces. He is now ensconced as my number two starter. That's exactly where he's ensconced!"

He looked out again at Casey to see him throw a straight, fast ball that landed in Monk's glove and sent smoke rising from home plate. Monk whipped off the glove and held his hand agonizedly. When the pain subsided he stared at the young pitcher disbelievingly. It was then and only then that picture and sound began to register in Mouth McGarry's mind. He suddenly thought about the last two pitches that he'd seen and his eyebrows shot up like elevators. Monk approached him, holding his injured hand.

"You see him?" Monk asked in an incredulous voice. "That kid? He picks up where Feller left off, I swear to God! He's got a curve, hook, knuckler, slider and a fast ball that almost went through my palm! He's got control like he uses radar. This is the best pitcher I ever caught in my life, Mouth!"

Mouth McGarry stood there as if mesmerized, staring at Casey who was walking slowly away from the mound. Monk tucked his catcher's mitt under his arm and started toward the dugout.

"I swear," he said as he walked, "I never seen anything like it. Fantastic. He pitches *like nothing human!*"

Mouth McGarry and Dr. Stillman looked at one another. Dr. Stillman's quiet blue eyes looked knowing and Mouth McGarry chewed furiously down the length of a piece of grass, his last bite taking in a quarter inch of his forefinger. He blew on it, waved it in the air and stuck it in his mouth as he turned toward Stillman, his voice shaking with excitement.

"Look, Grampa," Mouth said, "I want that boy! Understand? I'll have a contract drawn up inside of fifteen minutes. And don't give me no tough talk either! You brought him here on a try-out and that gives us first option."

"He's a robot, you know," Stillman began quietly.

Mouth grabbed him and spoke through clenched teeth. "Grampa," he said in a quiet fury, "don't ever say that to nobody! We'll just keep that in the family here." Then suddenly remembering, he looked around wildly for the blueprint, picked it up from the ground and shoved it in his shirt pocket. He saw Stillman looking at him.

"Would that be honest?" Stillman said, rubbing his jaw.

Mouth pinched his cheek and said, "You sweet old guy, you're looking at a desperate man. And if the baseball commissioner ever found out I was using a machine—I'd be dead. D-E-D! Dead, you know?" Mouth's face brightened into a grimace which vaguely brought to mind a smile when he saw Casey approaching. "I like your stuff, kid," Mouth said to him. "Now you go into the locker room and change your clothes." He turned to Stillman. "He wears clothes, don't he?"

"Oh, by all means," Stillman answered.

"Good," Mouth said, satisfied. "Then we'll go up to Beasley's office and sign the contract." He looked at the tall pitcher standing there and shook his head. "If you could pitch once a week like I just seen you pitch, the only thing that stands between us and a pennant is if your battery goes dead or you rust in the rain! As of right now, Mr. Casey—you're the number one pitcher of the Brooklyn Dodgers!"

Stillman smiled happily and Casey just looked impassive, no expression, no emotion, neither satisfied nor dissatisfied. He just stood there. Mouth hurried back to the dugout, took the steps three at a time and grabbed the phone.

"General Manager's office," he screamed into it. "Yeah!" In a moment he heard Beasley's voice. "Beasley?" he said. "Listen, Beasley, I want you to draw up a contract. It's for that left-hander. His name is Casey. That's right. Not just good, Beasley. Fantastic. Now you draw up that contract in a hurry." There was an angry murmur at the other end of the line. "Who do you think I'm giving orders to," Mouth demanded. He slammed the phone down then turned to look out toward the field.

Stillman and Casey were heading toward the dugout. Mouth rubbed his jaw pensively. Robot-shmobot, he said to himself. He's got a curve, knuckler, fast ball, slider, change of pace and hallelujah—he's got two arms!

He picked up one of Bertram Beasley's cigars off the ground, smoothed out the pleats and shoved it into his mouth happily. For the first time in many long and bleak months Mouth McGarry had visions of a National League pennant fluttering across his mind. So must John McGraw have felt when he got his first look at Walter Johnson or Muller Higgins, when George Herman Ruth came to him from the Boston Red Socks. And McGarry's palpitations were surely not unlike those of Marse Joseph McCarthy when a skinny Italian kid named DiMaggio ambled out into center field for the first time. Such was the bonfire of hope that was kindled in Mouth Mc-Garry's chest as he looked at the blank-faced, giant left-hander walking toward him, carrying on his massive shoulders, albeit invisibly, the fortunes of the Brooklyn Dodgers and Mrs. McGarry's son, Mouth!

It was a night game against St. Louis forty-eight hours later. The dressing room of the Brooklyn Dodgers was full of noise, clattering cleats, slammed locker doors, the plaintive protests of Bertram Beasley who was accusing the trainer of using too much liniment (at seventy-nine cents a bottle), and the deep, bullfrog profanity of Mouth McGarry who was all over the room, on every bench, in every corner, and in every head of hair.

"You sure he's got the signals down, Monk?" he asked his catcher for the fourteenth time.

Monk's eyes went up toward the ceiling and he said tiredly, "Yeah, boss. He knows them."

Mouth walked over to the pitcher who was just tying up his shoes. "Casey," he said urgently, wiping the sweat from his forehead, "if you forget them signals—you call time and bring Monk out to you, you understand? I don't want no cross-ups." He took out a large handkerchief and mopped his brow, then he pulled out a pill from his side pocket and plopped it into his mouth. "And above all," he cautioned his young pitcher, "—don't be nervous!"

Casey looked up at him puzzled. "Nervous?" he asked.

Stillman, who had just entered the room, walked over to them smiling. "Nervous, Casey," he explained, "ill at ease. As if one of your electrodes were—"

Mouth drowned him out loudly, "You know 'nervous,' Casey! Like as if there's two outs in the ninth, you're one up, and you're pitchin' against DiMaggio and he comes up to the plate lookin' intent!"

Casey stared at him deadpan. "That wouldn't make me nervous. I don't know anyone named DiMaggio."

"He don't know anyone named DiMaggio," Monk explained seriously to Mouth McGarry.

"I heard 'im," Mouth screamed at him. "I heard 'im!" He turned to the rest of the players, looked at his watch then bellowed out, "All right, you guys, let's get going!"

Monk took Casey's arm and pulled him off the bench and then out the door. The room resounded with the clattering cleats on concrete floor as the players left the room for the dugout above. Mouth McGarry stood alone in the middle of the room and felt a dampness settle all over him. He pulled out a sopping wet handkerchief and wiped his head again.

"This humidity," he said plaintively to Dr. Stillman who sat on the bench surveying him, "is killing me. I've never felt such dampness—I swear to God!"

Stillman looked down at Mouth's feet. McGarry was standing with one foot in a bucket of water.

"Mr. McGarry," he pointed to the bucket.

Mouth lifted up his foot sheepishly and shook it. Then he took out his bottle of pills again, popped two of them in his mouth, gulped them down and pointed apologetically to his stomach. "Nerves," he said. "Terrible nerves. I don't sleep at night. I keep seeing pennants before my eyes. Great big, red, white and blue pennants. All I can think about is knocking off the Giants and then taking four straight from the Yanks in the World Series." He sighed deeply. "But for that matter," he continued, "I'd like to knock off the Phillies and the Cards, too. Or the Braves or Cincinnati." A forlorn note crept into his voice now. "Or anybody when you come down to it!"

Dr. Stillman smiled at him. "I think Casey will come through for you, Mr. McGarry."

Mouth looked at the small white-haired man. "What have you got riding on this?" he asked. "What's your percentage?"

"You mean with Casey?" Stillman said. "Just scientific, that's all. Purely experimental. I think that Casey is a superman of a sort and I'd like that proven. Once I built a home economist. Marvelous cook. I gained forty-six pounds before I had to dismantle her. Now with Casey's skills, his strength and his accuracy, I realized he'd be a baseball pitcher. But in order to prove my point I had to have him pitch in competition. Also as an acid test, I had to have him pitch with absolutely the worst ball team I could find."

"That's very nice of you, Dr. Stillman," Mouth said. "I appreciate it."

"Don't mention it. Now shall we go out on the field?"

Mouth opened the door for him. "After you," he said.

Dr. Stillman went out and Mouth was about to follow him when he stopped dead, one eyebrow raised. "Wait a minute, dammit," he shouted. "The worst?" He started out after the old man. "You should have seen the Phillies in 1903!" he yelled after him.

An umpire screamed, "Play ball!" and the third baseman took a throw from the catcher then, rubbing up the ball, he carried it over to Casey on the mound, noticing in a subconscious section of his mind that this kid with the long arms and the vast shoulders had about as much spirit as a lady of questionable virtue on a Sunday morning after a long Saturday night. A few moments later, the third baseman cared very little about the lack of animation on Casey's features. This feeling was shared by some fourteen thousand fans, who watched the left-hander look dully in for a sign, then throw a side-arm fast ball that left them gasping and sent the entire dugout of the St. Louis Cardinals to their feet in amazement.

There are fast balls and fast balls, but nothing remotely resembling the white streak that shot out of Casey's left hand, almost invisibly toward the plate, had ever been witnessed. A similar thought ran through the mind of the St. Louis batter as he blinked at the sound of the ball hitting the catcher's mitt and took a moment to realize that the pitch had been made and he had never laid eyes on it.

This particular St. Louis batter was the first of twenty-five men to face Casey that evening. Eighteen of them struck out and only two of them managed to get to first base, one on a fluke single that was misjudged over first base. By the sixth inning most of the people in the stadium were on their feet, aware that they were seeing something special in the tall left-hander on the mound. And by the ninth inning when Brooklyn had won its first game in three weeks by a score of two to nothing, the stadium was in a frenzy.

There was also a frenzy of a sort in the Brooklyn dugout. The corners of Mouth McGarry's mouth tilted slightly upward in a grimace which the old team trainer explained later to a couple of mystified ballplayers was a "smile." Mouth hadn't been seen to smile in the past six years.

Bertram Beasley celebrated the event by passing out three brand new cigars and one slightly used one (to McGarry). But the notable thing about the Brooklyn dugout and later the locker room was that the ball team suddenly looked different. In the space of about two and a half hours, it had changed from some slogging, lead-footed, aging second-raters to a snappy, heads-up, confident looking crew of ball-players who had a preoccupation with winning. The locker room resounded with laughter and horse-play, excited shouting drifted out from the showers. All this in a room that for the past three years had been as loud and comical as a funeral parlor.

While wet towels sailed across the room and cleated shoes banged against locker doors, one man remained silent. This was the pitcher named Casey. He surveyed the commotion around him with a mild interest, but was principally concerned with unlacing his shoes. The only emotion he displayed was when Doc Barstow, the team trainer, started to massage his arm. He jumped up abruptly and yanked the arm away, leaving Barstow puzzled. Later on Barstow confided to Mouth McGarry that the kid's arm felt like a piece of tube steel. McGarry gulped, smiled nervously and asked Doc how his wife had been feeling. All this happened on the night of July 1st.

Three weeks later the Brooklyn Dodgers had moved from the cellar to fifth place in the National League. They had won twenty-three games in a row, seven of them delivered on a platter by one left-handed pitcher named Casey. Two of his ball games were no-hitters and his earned run average was by far the lowest not only in either League, but in the history of baseball. His name was on every tongue in the nation, his picture on every sports page, and contracts had already been signed so that he would be appearing on cereal boxes before the month was out. And as in life itself, winning begot winning. Even without Casey, the Dodgers were becoming a feared and formidable ball club. Weak and ineffectual bat-slappers, who had never hit more than .200 in their lives, were becoming Babe Ruths. Other pitchers who had either been too green or too decrepit were beginning to win ball games along with Casey. And there was a spirit now—an aggressiveness, a drive, that separated the boys from the pennant-winners and the Brooklyn Dodgers were potentially the latter. They looked it and they played it.

Mouth McGarry was now described as "that master strategist" and "a top field general" and, frequently, "the winningest manager of the year" in sports columns which had previously referred to him as "that cement-headed oaf who handles a ball club like a bull would handle a shrimp cocktail." The team was drawing more customers in single games than they'd garnered in months at a time during previous seasons. And the most delightful thing to contemplate was the fact that Casey, who had begun it all, looked absolutely invulnerable to fatigue, impervious to harm, and totally beyond the normal hazards of pitchers. He had no stiff arms, no sore elbows, no lapses of control, no nothing. He pitched like a machine and while it was mildly disconcerting, it was really no great concern that he also walked, talked and acted like a machine. There was no question about it. The Dodgers would have been in first place by mid-August at the very latest, if a shortstop on the Philadelphia Phillies had not hit a line ball directly at Casey on the mound which caught him just a few inches above his left eye.

The dull, sickening thud was the shot heard all around the borough and if anyone had clocked Mouth McGarry's run from the dugout to the mound where his ace left-hander was now sprawled face downward, two guys named Landy and Bannister would have been left in eclipse. Bertram Beasley, in his box seat in the grandstand, simply chewed off one quarter of his cigar and swallowed it, then fell off his seat in a dead faint.

The players grouped around Casey and Doc Barstow motioned for a stretcher. McGarry grabbed his arm and whispered at him as if already they were in the presence of the dead.

"Will he pull through, Doc? Will he make it?"

The team doctor looked grim. "I think we'd better get him to a hospital. Let's see what they say about him there."

Half the team provided an escort for the stretcher as it moved slowly off the field. It looked like a funeral cortège behind a recently deceased head of state with Mouth McGarry as the principal mourner. It was only then that he remembered to motion into the bullpen for a new pitcher, an eager young towhead out of the Southern Association League who had just been called up.

The kid ambled toward the mound. It was obvious that at this moment he wished he were back in Memphis, Tennessee, sorting black-eyed peas. He took the ball from the second baseman, rubbed it up, then reached down for the rosin bag. He rubbed his hands with the bag then rubbed the ball, then rubbed the bag then put down the ball, wound up and threw the rosin bag. As it turned out, this was his best pitch of the evening. Shortly thereafter he walked six men in a row and hit one man in the head. Luckily, it was a hotdog vendor in the bleachers so that no harm was done in terms of moving any of the men on base. This was taken care of by his next pitch to the number-four batter on the Philadelphia Phillies squad, who swung with leisurely grace at what the kid from Memphis referred to as his fast ball, and sent it on a seven-hundred-foot-trip over the center field fence, which took care of the men on the bases. The final score was thirteen to nothing in favor of the Phillies, but Mouth McGarry didn't even wait until the last out. With two outs in the ninth, he and Beasley ran out of the park and grabbed a cab. Beasley handed the driver a quarter and said, "Never mind the cops. Get to the hospital."

The hackie looked at the quarter then back toward Beasley and said, "This better be a rare mint, or I'll see to it that you have your baby in the cab!"

They arrived at the hospital twelve minutes later and pushed their way through a lobby full of reporters to get to an elevator and up to the floor where Casey had been taken for observation. They arrived in his room during the last stages of the examination. A nurse shushed them as they barged into the room.

"Boobie," McGarry gushed, racing toward the bed.

The doctor took off his stethescope and hung it around his neck. "You the father?" he asked Mouth.

"The father," McGarry chortled. "I'm closer than any father."

He noticed now for the first time that Dr. Stillman was sitting quietly in the corner of the room looking like a kindly old owl full of wisdom hidden under his feathers.

"Well, gentlemen, there's no fracture that I can see," the doctor announced professionally. "No concussion. Reflexes seem normal—"

Beasley exhaled sounding like a strong north-wind. "I can breathe again," he told everyone.

"All I could think of," Mouth said, "was there goes Casey! There goes the pennant! There goes the Series!" He shook his head forlornly, "And there goes my career."

The doctor picked up Casey's wrist and began to feel for the pulse. "Yes, Mr. Casey," he smiled benevolently down into the expressionless face and unblinking eyes, "I think you're in good shape. I'll tell you though, when I heard how the ball hit you in the temple I wondered to myself how—"

The doctor stopped talking. His fingers compulsively moved around the wrist. His eyes went wide. After a moment he opened up Casey's pajamas and sent now shaking fingers running over the chest area. After a moment he stood up, took out a handkerchief and wiped his face.

"What's the matter?" Mouth asked nervously. "What's wrong?"

The doctor sat down in a chair. "There's nothing wrong," he said softly. "Not a thing wrong. Everything's fine. It's just that—"

"Just that what?" Beasley asked.

The doctor pointed a finger toward the bed. "It is just that this man doesn't have any pulse. No heart beat." Then he looked up toward the ceiling. "This man," he said in a strained voice, "this man isn't alive."

There was absolute silence in the room marred only by the slump of Beasley's body as he slid quietly to the floor. No one paid any attention to him. It was Dr. Stillman who finally spoke.

"Mr. McGarry," he said in a quiet, firm voice, "I do believe it'll have to come out now."

Beasley opened his eyes. "All right, you sonofabitch, McGarry, what are you trying to pull off?"

Mouth looked around the room as if searching for an extra bed. He looked ill. "Beasley," he said plaintively, "you ain't gonna like this. But it was Casey or it was nothing. God, what a pitcher! And he was the only baseball player I ever managed who didn't eat nothing."

Stillman cleared his throat and spoke to the doctor. "I think you should know before you go any further that Casey has no pulse or heart beat . . . because he hasn't any heart. He's a robot."

There was the sound of another slump as Bertram Beasley fell back unconscious. This time he didn't move.

"A *what*?" the doctor asked incredulously.

"That's right," Stillman said. "A robot."

The doctor stared at Casey on the bed who stared right back at him. "Are you sure?" the doctor asked in a hushed voice.

"Oh, by all means. I built him."

The doctor slowly removed his coat and then took off his tie. He marched toward the bed with his eyes strangely wide and bright. "Casey," he announced, "get up and strip. Hear me? Get up and strip."

Casey got up and stripped and twenty minutes later the doctor had opened the window and was leaning out breathing in the evening air. Then he turned, removed his stethescope from around his neck and put it in his black bag. He took the blood pressure equipment from the night-stand and added this to the bag. He made a mental note to check the X rays as soon as they came out, but knew this would be gratuitous because it was all very, very evident. The man on the bed wasn't a man at all. He was one helluva speciman, but a man he wasn't! The doctor lit a cigarette and looked across the room.

"Under the circumstances," he said, "I'm afraid I must notify the baseball commissioner. That's the only ethical procedure."

"What do you have to be ethical about it for?" McGarry challenged him. "What the hell are you—a Giant fan?"

The doctor didn't answer. He took the twenty or thirty sheets of paper that he'd been making notes on and rammed them in his pocket. He mentally ran down the list of medical societies and organizations that would have to be informed of this. He also devised the opening three or four paragraphs to a monumental paper he'd write for a medical journal on the first mechanical man. He was in for a busy time. He carried his black bag to the door, smiled and went out, wondering just how the American Medical Association would react to this one. The only sound left in the room was Beasley's groaning, until Mc-Garry walked over to Casey on the bed.

"Casey," he said forlornly, "would you move over?"

The Daily Mirror had it first because one of the interns in the maternity ward was really a leg man for them. But the two wire services picked it up twenty minutes later and by six the following morning the whole world knew about Casey—the mechanical man. Several scientists were en route from Europe, and Dr. Stillman and Casey were beleaguered in a New York hotel room by an army of photographers and reporters. Three missile men at Cape

Canaveral sent up a fabulous rocket that hit the moon dead-eye only to discover that the feat made page twelve of the afternoon editions because the first eleven pages were devoted exclusively to a meeting to be held by the commissioner of baseball, who had announced he would make a decision on the Casey case by suppertime.

At four-thirty that afternoon the commissioner sat behind his desk, drumming on it with the end of a pencil. A secretary brought him in a folder filled with papers and in the brief moment of the office door opening, he could see the mob of reporters out in the corridor.

"What about the reporters?" the secretary asked him.

Mouth McGarry, sitting in a chair close to the desk, made a suggestion at this point as to what might be done to the reporters or, more specifically, what they could do to themselves. The secretary looked shocked and left the room. The commissioner leaned back in his chair.

"You understand, McGarry," he said, "that I'm going to have to put this out for publication. Casey must definitely be suspended."

Bertram Beasley, sitting on a couch across the room, made a little sound deep in his throat, but stayed conscious.

"Why?" Mouth demanded noisily.

The commissioner pounded a fist on the desk top. "Because he's a robot, Goddamn it," he said for the twelfth time that hour.

Mouth spread out his palms. "So he's a robot," he said simply.

Once again the commissioner picked up a large manual. "Article six, section two, the Baseball Code," he said pontifically. "I quote: 'A team should consist of nine men' end of quote. Men, understand, McGarry? Nine *men*. Not robots."

Beasley's voice was a thin little noise from the couch. "Commissioner," he said weakly. "To all intents and purposes—he *is* human." Then he looked across the room at the tall pitcher who stood in the shadows practically unnoticed. "Casey, talk to him. Tell him about yourself."

Casey swallowed. "What—what should I say," he asked hesitantly.

"See," Mouth shouted. "He talks as good as me. And he's a whole helluva lot smarter than most of the mutton-heads I got on my ball team!"

The commissioner's fist pounded on the desk. *"He is not human!"*

Again the weak voice of desperation from the couch. "How human do you want him?" the general manager asked. "He's got arms, legs, a face. He talks—"

"And no heart," the commissioner shouted. "He doesn't even own a heart. How could he be human without a heart?"

McGarry's voice absolutely dripped with unassailable logic and fundamental truth. "Beasley don't have a heart neither," he said, "and he owns forty per cent of the club."

The commissioner pushed the papers away from him and put the flat of his hands down on the desk. This was a gesture of finality and it fitted perfectly the judicial tone of his voice. "That's it, gentlemen," he announced. "He doesn't have a heart. That means he isn't human, and that's a clear violation of the baseball code. Therefore he doesn't play."

The door opened and Dr. Stillman walked quietly into the room in time to hear the last words of this proclamation. He waved at Casey who waved back. Then he turned to the commissioner.

"Mr. Commissioner," he said.

The commissioner stopped halfway to his feet and looked at the old man. "Now what?" he asked tiredly.

Stillman walked over to the desk. "Supposing," he asked, "we gave him a heart? If that essentially is the only thing that makes him different from the norm, I believe I could operate and supply him with a mechanical heart."

"That's thinking!" McGarry shrieked into the room.

Beasley inched forward on the couch and took out a cigar. The commissioner sat back and looked very, very thoughtful. "This is irregular. This is highly irregular." Then he picked up the telephone and asked to speak to the examining physician who had sent in the report in the first place. "Doctor," he asked, "relative to the Casey matter, if he were to be given a mechanical heart—would you classify him as—what I mean is—would you call him a—" Then he held the phone close to his face, nodding into it. "Thank you very much, Doctor."

The commissioner looked across the room at Casey. He drummed on the desk top with the pencil, puckered up his lips and made smacking sounds inside of his mouth. McGarry took out his bottle of pills and plopped three of them into his mouth.

"All right," the commissioner announced. "*With* a heart, I'll give him a temporary okay until the League meeting in November. Then we'll have to take it up again. The other clubs are gonna scream bloody murder!"

Beasley struggled to his feet. The look of massive relief on his face shown like a beacon. "It's all settled then," he said. "Casey here needs an accreditation as being human and this requires a simple—" He stopped, looking over toward Stillman. "Simple?" he asked.

"Relatively," Stillman answered.

Beasley nodded. "A simple operation having to do with a mechanical heart." He walked across the room to the door and opened it. The reporters, milling around, stopped talking instantly. "Gentlemen," Beasley called out to them, "you may quote me."

The reporters made a beeline for the door and within a moment had filled up the room.

"You may quote me, gentlemen," Beasley repeated when the room was quiet once again. "The mighty Casey will be back in the line-up within forty-eight hours." He threw another questioning look at Stillman. "Forty-eight hours?"

"About," Stillman answered quietly.

Questions shot around the room like bolts of lightning and for the next few moments McGarry, Beasley and Casey were innundated by notebooks and cigarette smoke. Then the room started to empty. Mouth McGarry took a position close to the desk, stuck a cigar in his mouth, lit it, took a deep drag and held it out away from his body, gently flicking ashes on the floor.

"Gentlemen," he announced, "as manager of the Brooklyn Dodgers, I want to tell you, and since I was the man who discovered Casey—"

The reporters rapidly left the room followed by the commissioner and his secretary, followed by Casey and Stillman.

"It behooves me to tell you gentlemen," Mouth continued, wetting his lips over the word "behooves" and wondering to himself where he got the word. "It behooves me to make mention of the fact that the Brooklyn Dodgers are the team to beat. We've got the speed, the stamina," he recollected now the Pat O'Brien speech in a Knute Rockne picture, "the vim, the vigor, the vitality—"

He was unaware of the door slamming shut and unaware that Bertram Beasley was the only other man in the room. "And with this kind of stuff," he continued, in the Knute Rockne voice, "the National League pennant and the World Series and—"

"McGarry," Beasley yelled at him.

Mouth started as if suddenly waking from a dream.

Beasley rose from the couch. "Why don't you drop dead?" He walked out of the room, leaving Mouth all by himself, wondering how Pat O'Brien wound up that speech in the locker room during the half-time of that vital Army-Notre Dame game.

How either McGarry or Bertram Beasley got through the next twenty-odd hours was a point of conjecture with both of them. Mouth emptied his bottle of nerve pills and spent a sleepless night pacing his hotel room floor. Beasley could recall only brief moments of consciousness between swoons which occurred every time the phone rang.

The following night the team was dressing in the locker room. They were playing the first of a five-game series against the New York Giants and McGarry had already devised nine different batteries, then torn them all up. He now sat on a bench surveying his absolutely silent ballplayers. There was not a sound. At intervals each pair of eyes would turn toward the phone on the wall. Beasley had already phoned Dr. Stillman's residence seven times that evening and received no answer. He was on the phone now, talking to the long distance operator in New Jersey.

"Yeah," Beasley said into the phone. "Yeah, well thank you very much, operator."

Mouth and the rest of the players waited expectantly. "Well?" Mouth asked. "How is he?"

Beasley shook his head. "I don't know. The operator still can't get an answer."

Monk, the big catcher, rose from the bench. "Maybe he's right in the middle of the operation," he suggested.

Mouth whirled around at him, glaring. "So he's in the middle of the operation! Whatsa matter, he can't use one hand to pick up a phone?" He looked up at the clock on the wall then jutted his jaw fiercely, his eyes scanning the bench. "We can't wait no longer," he announced. "I got to turn in a battery. Corrigan," he said pointing toward one of the players, "you'll pitch tonight. And now the rest of you guys!" He stuck his hands in his back pockets and paced back and forth in front of them in a rather stylized imitation of Pat O'Brien.

"All right, you guys," he said grimly. "All right, you guys!" He stopped pacing and pointed toward the door. "That's the enemy out there," he said, his voice quivering a little. "That's the New York Giants." He spoke the words as if they were synonymous with a social disease. "And while we're out there playing tonight"—again his voice quivered—"there's a big fellah named Casey lying on a table, struggling to stay alive."

Tears shone in Monk's eyes as the big catcher got a mental picture of a courageous kid lying on a hospital table. Gippy Resnick, the third baseman, sniffed and then honked into a handkerchief as a little knot of sentiment tightened up his throat. Bertram Beasley let out a sob as he thought about what the attendance record was, six weeks B.C.—before Casey—and did some more projecting on what it would be without Casey. Mouth McGarry walked back and forth before the line of players.

"I know," he said, his voice tight and strained. "I know that his last words before that knife went into his chest were—'Go up there, Dodgers, and win one for the big guy!'."

The last words of this speech were choked by the tears that rolled down McGarry's face and the sob that caught in his own chest.

The street door to the locker room opened and Dr. Stillman came in, followed by Casey. But all the players were watching Mouth McGarry, who had now moved into his big finale scene.

"I want to tell you something, guys! From now on"— he sniffed loudly—"from now on there's gonna be a ghost in that dugout. Everytime you pick up a bat, look over to where Casey used to sit—because he's gonna be there in spirit rooting for us, cheering for us, yellin', 'Go Dodgers, go!' "—McGarry turned and looked at Casey, who was smiling at him. Mouth nodded perfunctorily. "Hello there, Casey," he said and turned back to the team. "Now I'm gonna tell you something else about that big guy. This fellah has a heart. Not a real heart, maybe, but this fellah that's lyin' there with a hole in his chest—"

Mouth's lower jaw dropped seven inches, as he turned very slowly to look at Casey. He had no chance to say anything, however, because the team has pushed him aside as they rushed toward the hero, shaking his hand, pounding him on the back, pulling, grabbing, shouting at him. Mouth spent a moment recovering and then screamed, "All right, knock it off! Let's have quiet! Quiet! QUIET!" He pulled players away from Casey and finally stood in front of the big pitcher. "Well?" he asked.

Stillman smiled. "Go ahead, Casey. Tell him."

It was then that everyone in the room noticed Casey's face. He was smiling. It was a big smile. A broad smile. An enveloping smile. It went across his face and up and down. It shone in his eyes. "Listen, Mr. McGarry," he said proudly. He pointed a thumb at his chest and Mouth put his ear there. He could hear the steady tick, tick, tick.

Mouth stepped back and shouted excitedly. "You got a heart!"

There was a chorus of delighted exclamation and comment from all the players and Beasley, poised for a faint, decided against it.

"And look at that smile," Stillman said over the shouting. "That's the one thing I couldn't get him to do before —smile!"

Casey threw his arm around the old man. "It's wonderful. It's just wonderful. Now I feel—I feel—like—togetherness!"

The team roared their approval and Bertram Beasley mounted a rubbing-table, cupping his hands like a megaphone, and shouted, "All right, Dodgers, out on the field. Let's go, team. Casey starts tonight. The new Casey!"

The team thundered out on to the field, pushing Mouth McGarry out of the way and blotting out the first part of the speech which had begun, "All right, you guys, with vim, vigor and vital—" He never got to finish the speech because Monk, Resnick and a utility infielder had carried him with their momentum out the door and up to the dugout.

When Casey's name was announced as the starter for the Dodgers that night the crowd let out a roar that dwarfed any thunder ever heard in or around the environs of New York City. And when Casey stepped out on the field and headed toward the mound, fifty-seven thousand eight hundred and thirty-three people stood up and applauded as one, and it was only the second baseman who, as he carried the ball over to the pitcher, noticed that there were tears in Casey's eyes and an expression on his face that made him pause. True, he'd never seen *any* expression on Casey's face before, but this one made him stop and look over his shoulder as he went back to his base.

The umpire shouted, "Play ball," and the Dodgers began the running stream of chatter that always prefaced the first pitch. Monk, behind the plate, made a signal and then held up his glove as a target. Start with a fast ball, he thought. Let them know what they're up against, jar them a little bit. Confuse them. Unnerve them. That was the way Monk planned his strategy behind the plate. Not that much strategy was needed, when Casey was on the mound, but it was always good to show the big guns first. Casey nodded, went into his wind-up and threw. Twelve seconds later a woman in a third-floor apartment three blocks away had her bedroom window smashed by a baseball that had traveled in the neighborhood of seven hundred feet out of Tebbet's Field.

Meanwhile, back at the field, the crowd just sat there silently as the lead-off batter of the New York Giants ambled around the base path heading home to the outstretched hands of several fellow Giants greeting him after his lead-off home run.

Mouth McGarry at this moment felt that he would never again suffer a stab of depression such as the one that now intruded into his head. He would recall later that his premonition was quite erroneous. He would feel stabs of depressions in innings number two, three and four that would make that first stab of depression seem like the after effect of a Miltown tablet. That's how bad it got forty-five minutes later, when Casey had allowed nine hits, had walked six men, had thrown two wild pitches, and had muffed a pop fly to the mound, which, McGarry roared to the bench around him, "could have been caught by a palsied Civil War veteran who lost an arm at Gettysburg."

In the seventh inning Mouth McGarry took his fifth walk over to the mound and this time didn't return to the bench till he'd motioned to the bullpen for Casey's relief—a very eager kid, albeit a nervous one, who chewed tobacco going to the mound and got violently sick as he crossed the third-base line because he swallowed a piece. Coughing hard, he arrived at the mound and took the ball from Mouth McGarry. Casey solemnly shoved his mitt into his hip pocket and took the long walk back toward the showers.

At ten minutes to midnight the locker room had been emptied. All the players save Casey had gone back to the hotel. Bertram Beasley had left earlier—on a stretcher in the sixth inning. In the locker room were a baseball manager who produced odd grunts from deep within his throat and kept shaking his head back and forth—and a kindly white-haired old man who built robots. Casey came out of the shower, wrapped in a towel. He smiled gently at Mouth and then went over to his locker where he proceeded to dress.

"Well?" Mouth shouted at him. "Well? One minute he's three Lefty Groves, the next minute he's the cousin to every New York Giant who ever lived. He's a tanker. He's a nothing. All right—you wanna tell me, Casey? You wanna explain? You might start by telling me how one man can throw nine pitched balls and give up four singles, two doubles, a triple and two home runs!"

The question remained unanswered. Stillman looked toward Casey and said very softly, "Shall I tell him?"

Casey nodded apologetically.

Stillman turned toward McGarry. "Casey has a heart," he said quietly.

Mouth fumed. "So? Casey has a heart! So I know he's gotta heart! So this ain't news, prof! Tell me something that is!"

"The thing is," Casey said in his first speech over three sentences since McGarry had met him. "The thing is, Mr. McGarry, I just couldn't strike out those poor fellahs. I didn't have it in me to do that—to hurt their feelings. I felt—I felt compassion!" He looked toward Stillman as if for confirmation.

Stillman nodded. "That's what he's got, Mr. McGarry. Compassion. See how he smiles?"

Casey grinned obediently and most happily, and Stillman returned his smile. "You see, Mr. McGarry," Stillman continued. "You give a person a heart—particularly someone like Casey, who hasn't been around long enough to understand things like competitiveness or drive or ego. "Well," he shrugged, "that's what happens."

Mouth sat down on the bench, unscrewed the bottle of pills and found it was empty. He threw the bottle over his shoulder. "That's what happens to *him,*" he said. "Shall I tell you what happens to me? I go back to being a manager of nine gleeps so old that I gotta rub them down with formaldehyde and revive them in between innings." He suddenly had a thought and looked up at Casey. "Casey," he asked, "don't you feel any of that compassion for the Brooklyn Dodgers?"

Casey smiled back at him. "I'm sorry, Mr. McGarry," he said. "It's just that I can't strike out fellahs. I can't bring myself to hurt their careers. Dr. Stillman thinks I should go into social work now. I'd like to help people. Right, Dr. Stillman?"

"That's right, Casey," Stillman answered.

"Are you going?" Casey asked McGarry as he saw the manager head for the door.

Mouth nodded.

"Well good-by, Mr. McGarry," Casey said. "And thank you for everything."

Mouth turned to him. The grin on his face was that of dying humanity all over the world. "Don't mention it," he said.

He sighed deeply and walked out to the warm August evening that awaited him and the black headlines on a newspaper stand just outside the stadium that said, "I told you so" at him, even though the lettering spelled out, "CASEY SHELLED FROM MOUND." A reporter stood on the corner, a guy McGarry knew slightly.

"What about it, McGarry?" the reporter asked. "What do you do for pitchers now?"

Mouth looked at him dully. "I dunno," he sighed. "I just feel them one by one and whoever's warm——"

He walked past the reporter and disappeared into the night, a broken-nosed man with sagging shoulders who thought he heard the rustle of pennants in the night air, and then realized it was three shirts on a clothesline that stretched across two of the adjoining buildings.

From Rod Serling's closing narration, "The Mighty Casey," The Twilight Zone, scheduled for telecast March 25, 1960, CBS Television Network.

A BASEBALL FIELD—LONG ANGLE SHOT
It is empty and in absolute quiet.

NARRATOR'S VOICE
Once upon a time there was a major
league team called the Brooklyn

Dodgers who during the last year
of their existence as a ball team
wound up in last place and shortly
thereafter wound up in oblivion.
They are rarely if ever mentioned
in these parts again. Rumor has
it that a ball club on the West
Coast is the residue of what was
left of the original ball club.

(a pause)

And on occasion in a dark bar off
Flatbush Avenue, someone might
whisper the name of a certain pitcher
with an exceptional left hand. Somebody else will softly murmur the
question—whatever happened to the
mighty Casey?

(a pause)

No, you won't find any of the answers
in the records. Though they are
available should anyone be interested
by checking under "B" for baseball
in the Twilight Zone!

FADE TO BLACK

Escape Clause

Walter Bedeker lay on his bed waiting for the doctor. He wore a heavy, wool bathrobe over heavy wool pajamas, and had a heavy wool scarf wrapped tightly around his head and knotted under the chin in a giant bow. On the bedstand next to him was a tray full of bottles. There were pills, lotions, antibiotics, nasal sprays, throat sprays, ear drops, nose drops, three boxes of Kleenex and a book titled, *How To Be Happy Though Bedridden*. He stared dourly up at the ceiling then cocked an irritated eye toward the bedroom door, beyond which he could hear his wife's footsteps walking from kitchen to living room.

Ethel his wife was healthy. Oh God, she was healthy! Like a horse was Ethel. Never even had a cold. But he, Walter Bedeker, went from crisis to crisis, ailment to ailment, agonizing pain to agonizing pain.

Walter Bedeker was forty-four years old. He was afraid of the following: death, disease, other people, germs, drafts and everything else. He had one interest in life, and that was Walter Bedeker; one preoccupation, the life and well being of Walter Bedeker; one abiding concern about society, if Walter Bedeker should die, how would it survive without him. In short, he was a gnome-faced little man who clutched at disease the way most people hunger for security.

Ethel entered his room for the fifth time that hour to even out his blankets, fluff up his pillow. He looked at her jaundice-eyed and didn't say anything except to groan slightly when she helped him put his head back down on the pillow.

"Head still ache, darling?" Ethel asked him.

"Ache, Ethel, is not the word for it," he told her through a taut mouth. "Ache is a mild inconvenience. What I have is an agony. What I have is a living torture!"

Ethel made a brave attempt at a sympathetic smile. Walter never talked of his ailments in anything less than superlatives and this was his fifth stay-in-bed that month. The door chimes rang and she was unable to keep the look of relief from crossing her features. Walter recognized it instantly.

"Can't stand being in the room with me, can you," he said to her. "Sick people bore you, don't they?" He turned away to look at the wall to his right. "That is the tragedy of illness," he said to the wall. "The fleeting compassion of your so-called loved ones!"

"Oh, Walter—" Ethel began, and then stopped. She shrugged resignedly and went to answer the front door.

The doctor was waiting there with his black bag and he followed Ethel into the bedroom.

"Well, how are you feeling today, Mr. Bedeker?" he asked. The doctor was tired and his feet hurt. He hated house calls unless they were emergencies and Walter Bedeker's beckonings were never emergencies. He had difficulty keeping the tiredness out of his voice.

"How do I look?" Bedeker barked at him.

The doctor smiled at him and said, "Rather well, as a matter of fact."

Bedeker's face screwed up like a persimmon and mimicked him fiercely. "Rather well, as a matter of fact, huh? Well I can assure you, doctor, I'm not rather well. I'm not in the least bit well. I'm a very sick man. Which you'll soon discover once you examine me. But I want you to tell me the worst. I don't want any cushioning. I'm not a coward, doctor."

"I'm sure you aren't. Hold your arm out, Mr. Bede-ker. I'd like to take your pressure first."

Bedeker thrust out a remarkably well muscled arm for a man his age and the doctor wrapped the pressure cloth around it.

Ten minutes later he was putting most of his impedimenta back in the bag while Bedeker stared at him glumly.

"Well, doctor?"

The doctor closed the bag and turned to Bedeker without speaking.

"I asked you a question, doctor. How bad is it?"

"It isn't bad at all," the doctor said. "As a matter of fact, it's quite good. You have no temperature. Pressure normal. Respiration normal. Heart action normal. No infection. Throat clear. Nasal passages clear. Ears clear."

"What about the pains in my back and side? What about four sleepless nights in a row? What about *that*?" Bedeker shouted triumphantly.

The doctor shook his head. "What about that? 'That,' Mr. Bedeker, is psychosomatic!"

Bedeker's eyes grew large. "Psychosomatic? You're trying to tell me that I'm sick only in the mind?"

"Something like that, Mr. Bedeker," the doctor answered quietly. "There's nothing wrong with you, really, except the ailments you manufacture for yourself. Your pains, Mr. Bedeker, are imaginary. Your inability to sleep is a case of nerves—but nothing more. In short, Mr. Bedeker, you're a very healthy man!"

Walter Bedeker smiled sadly at his favorite confidant, the wall on the right, and talked to it, occasionally jerking his head toward the doctor.

"See? This is a doctor. Four years pre-med. Four years medical school. Two years internship. Two years residency. And what is he? I ask you, what is he?" Then he shouted, "A quack!"

The doctor had to smile in spite of himself. Ethel came in on tiptoe, and whispered to the doctor, "What's the prognosis?"

Bedeker shouted, "Don't ask *him*. The man's an idiot!"

"Walter, darling," Ethel said patiently, "don't excite yourself."

"Don't whisper," Bedeker shouted. "You're looking at half of my troubles right there," he said to the doctor. "This woman. This awful woman who runs around whispering all day long to make me *think* I'm sick even if I'm not. And I *am,*" he added quickly. "I'm lying here at death's door and who's ushering me out? A quack and this whispering woman without a mind!"

"I'll call tomorrow, Mrs. Bedeker," the doctor said jovially.

"There'll be no need to call," Bedeker answered. "Just come on over with the death certificate and fill it out."

"Oh, Walter—" Ethel said piteously.

"Don't drench me with those crocodile tears of yours, idiot," Bedeker screamed at her. "She'd be so happy to get rid of me, doctor, I just can't tell you!"

The doctor was no longer smiling as he went out, followed by Ethel. At the front door he looked at her very closely. She must have been a very attractive woman in her day. God, to be married to that man for as long as she'd been married to him!

"How is he, doctor?" Ethel asked.

"Mrs. Bedeker," the doctor said, "your husband is one of the healthiest patients I have. If he were up in front of me for an exam to get into the combat Marines, I'd pass him with flying colors."

Ethel shook her head dubiously. "He's sick most of the time. He won't let me open a window in the house. He says for every cubic foot of air there are eight million, nine hundred thousand germs."

The doctor threw back his head and laughed. "He's probably right."

Ethel added worriedly, "And he's just quit his job. The fifth job he's quit since the first of the year. He says they make him work in a draft."

The doctor stopped laughing and looked at this small, comely woman in front of him. "Mrs. Bedeker," he said softly, "there isn't a thing in the world I can do for your husband. Or any other doctor for that matter—except, perhaps, a psychiatrist."

Ethel's hand went to her mouth in a shocked gesture. "A psychiatrist," she said.

The doctor nodded. "His trouble is in his mind. This awful fear of disease. This phobia about death. I suppose I'm oversimplifying it when I say there's nothing wrong with him because in a sense there really is. This constant worrying about himself is an illness of a sort. Has he always been this frightened?"

"Ever since I can remember," said Ethel. "When he was courting me he told me he was in the last stages of T.B. and only had a week to live." She looked away reminiscently and sadly. "I only married him because I felt so sorry for him—!" She bit her lip. "What I meant, doctor—"

The doctor patted her on the arm and said, "I understand. I'll give you a call tomorrow." He looked closely at her again, reached in his pocket for a pad and scribbled down a prescription. "Here," he said, handing it to her. "You look a little run-down yourself. This is for vitamins."

Bedeker's voice came shrieking from the bedroom. "Ethel! There's a draft in here and I feel a coma coming on!"

"Yes, darling," Ethel hurriedly called. "I'll be right in."

"Don't forget about the vitamins," said the doctor, wincing a little at the sound of Bedeker's voice. "Goodby, Mrs. Bedeker."

Ethel shut the door behind him and rushed back into the bedroom.

Bedeker lay on the bed, his head off the pillow, and waved weakly toward the window to his left. "Ethel," he whined at her, "there's freezing air blasting into the room!"

The window was open about a fifth of an inch. As she put it down, Bedeker half-rose in bed.

"Do you know how many germs come in one cubic foot of air, Ethel?"

Under her breath she repeated the figure as he called it out.

"Eight million, nine hundred thousand!" He lowered his head back to the pillow. "I know you want me gone and that's why you leave windows open all over the place, but as a point of decency, Ethel, couldn't you do it more subtly?"

Ethel smoothed out his blankets. "The doctor said you needed some air. He said it was stuffy in here." She patted his hand which he drew away sharply.

He suddenly saw the prescription in her other hand. "What's this?" Bedeker said, yanking it out of her fingers. "Where'd you get this? I'm not sick, but he gives you a prescription for medicine for me. Nothing wrong with me and while I lie here helpless, he's out there telling you that I've got a life expectancy of twenty minutes." He puckered up his mouth like a prune. "Don't deny it, Ethel. Kindly don't deny it. I smelled the collusion the moment he left the room!"

Ethel's eyes closed as a wave of weakness hit her. Then she took a deep breath. "It is for vitamins, Walter, for *me*."

Bedeker bolted upright in bed. "Vitamins? For *you*." Then he turned to the wall and spoke to it, nodding familiarly at it. "I lie here while the life seeps out of me, and that quack prescribes medicines for my wife. See? I'm dying and she gets vitamins!"

He broke into a spasm of coughing. When Ethel tried to pat his back he pushed her away, then very limply and weakly he lay back down on the bed, shook his head and closed his eyes.

"Never mind, Ethel. Go on, get out of here. Let me die in peace."

"All right, Walter," Ethel said softly.

"*What?*" Bedeker shouted.

This time it was Ethel's eyes that closed. "I meant," she whispered, "I'll let you alone, Walter, so you can take a little nap."

He lay there quietly for a moment and then suddenly jumped up and sat on the edge of the bed. "I can't nap," he squealed. "Why does a man have to die anyway? I asked you a question, Ethel. Why does a man have to die?" He got out of bed and went to the window, feeling the sash at the bottom for any errant air that might intrude. "The world goes on for millions and millions of

years and how long is a man's life?" He held up two
fingers. "This much! A drop. A microscopic fragment.
Why can't a man live five hundred years? Or a thousand
years? Why does he have to die almost the minute he's
born?"

"I'm sure I don't know, dear."

"No, you wouldn't. Go on, get out of here, Ethel."

"Yes, dear," she said, and escaped into the living room
with the tremendous sense of relief she always felt after
getting out of Water Bedeker's presence. Today had been
one of the worst of days. He had called the doctor four
times that morning, then had Ethel phone the hospital to
check on the availability of an oxygen tent. He had insisted right after lunch that she phone the janitor to come
and check the heating pipes. The janitor had arrived and
Walter had immediately engaged him with a running
broadside from the bed as the janitor pounded on the hot
water pipes and steam and damp heat floated into the
room.

"You want heat, Mr. Bedeker?" the janitor had said to
him gleefully. "In about twenty minutes, it'll be about a
hundred and five in here. So heat you'll get!"

Livid with rage at the noise of the janitor's pounding, Bedeker had shouted at him, "Ape! Get out of here.
If I'm to die, at least I'll die in comfort and peace. Go
on, get out of here!"

The janitor surveyed his principal irritation in an apartment house of eighty-three families. "Well, if you do die,
Bedeker," he'd said, "—and you go where you're goin'—
as far as the temperature goes, you ain't gonna be able
to tell the difference!"

Now Ethel felt the result of the janitor's promise. The
apartment was stuffy beyond belief. She opened up one of
the living room windows and let the cool, fall air ripple
over her hot, tired flesh. But she could still hear Walter
Bedeker's running monologue from the bedroom.

"It's a crime for a man to live such a short span of
years. An absolute crime," Bedeker's muffled voice said.

Ethel went into the tiny kitchen, shut the door and
poured herself a cup of coffee.

Walter Bedeker sat propped up in bed looking at his

reflection in the dresser mirror across the room. "A crime," he repeated. "What I wouldn't give! What I wouldn't give to live a decent number of years. Two hundred. Three hundred." He heaved a deep sigh and shook his head.

A voice, deep, resonant, with a chuckle in it, said, "Why not five or six hundred?"

Bedeker nodded agreeably. "Why not? Or a thousand. What a miserable thing to contemplate. A handful of years, then an eternity in a casket down under the ground. The dark, cold ground!"

"With worms yet," the voice answered him.

"Of course, with worms," Bedeker said. Then his eyes grew wide as suddenly across the room, materializing rather rapidly in the bedroom chair, he saw a large, fat man in a dark suit. Bedeker gulped, gaped, blinked his eyes and then just stared.

The gentleman smiled and nodded. "I subscribe to your views wholly, Mr. Bedeker," he said. "I mean wholly."

Bedeker continued to stare at him and said, "I'm delighted. And who might you be?"

"Cadwallader's my name" the gentleman answered. "At least I'm using it this month. It has a nice feeling on the tongue."

Bedeker surreptitiously looked around the room, checking the door, the window, then took a quick look under the bed. Then he looked at the man accusingly. "How did you get in?"

"Oh, I've never been gone," Cadwallader said. "I've been here for some time." Then he leaned forward in the manner of a man about to start his business. "I'll be brief, Mr. Bedeker," he said. "You look like a man with a nose for a bargain. I'd like to make a proposition to you. We each have something the other wants, and that seems a relatively solid basis for a bargain."

Bedeker's voice was coolly appraising. "Do we? What in the world do you have that I could possibly want?"

The fat man smiled and lit a cigarette, then he sat back comfortably. "Oh, many things, Mr. Bedeker," he said. "You'd be surprised. Many things. Varied and delightful."

Bedeker studied the man's face. An odd face, he reflected. Fat, but not unpleasant. Nice white teeth, even though the eyes were a little shiny and wild. Bedeker scratched his jaw thoughtfully.

"What do I have that could remotely interest you?"

Cadwallader's smile was deprecating. "Actually a minor item," he said. "Smaller than minor. Insignificant. Microscopic." He held up two fat, little fingers. "Teensy weensy!"

The two men's eyes locked.

"What did you say your name was?" Bedeker asked.

"What's in a name, Mr. Bedeker?" Cadwallader replied ingratiatingly. "Just a question of semantics—language. A stretch of words, really. For example, what is it you want? You want an extended life span. You want a few hundred years to play around with. Now some people would call it immortality of a sort. But why give it that kind of description? Why make it sound so imposing. Let's call it—the two of us—let's call it some additional free time! After all what are a few hundred years or a few thousand years?"

Bedeker swallowed. "A few . . . *thousand*?"

"Or five thousand or ten thousand—" Cadwallader threw the numbers into the breach like a used car salesman bringing up his heavy artillery. "The world will go on ad infinitum, so what's a few thousand years more or less, give or take, add or subtract."

Bedeker rose warily from the bed and studied the fat man. "This little item, Mr. Cadwallader, that I am to give you in exchange—what do you call that?"

Cadwallader gave him a little Santa Claus wink. "What *do* we call that?" he asked. "Let's see! We can call it a little piece of your make-up. A little crumb off the crust of your structure. A fragment of an atom from your being." His smile persisted, but it never quite reached his eyes. "Or, we might call it a—"

"Or a soul!" Bedeker shrieked at him triumphantly.

The smile on Cadwallader's face was positively beatific. "Or that," he said softly. "After all, what is it? And when you're gone, thousands of years hence—what do you need it for?"

Walter Bedeker stood up and pointed a wavering finger in the direction of Mr. Cadwallader. *"You're the Devil,"* he announced.

Cadwallader bowed slightly from the giant equator that was his waist and said modestly, "I'm at your service. How about it, Mr. Bedeker? Why not? A partnership of a sort. You deed me over your so-called soul and I give you immortality. Life everlasting—or as long as you want it to be everlasting. And indestructibility, Mr. Bedeker. Think of it! Complete indestructibility. Nothing can ever hurt you!"

Bedeker looked off dreamily. "Nothing can hurt me? And I can live forever?"

Cadwallader smiled and said, "Why not? Certainly forever. Again, Mr. Bedeker, just terms. And everything's relative. For you it's forever. For me, it's just a walk around the block. But we're *both* satisfied."

Bedeker stood there lost in thought and Mr. Cadwallader walked over to his elbow. His voice was soft and gentle, but also rich with promise.

"Think of it," Cadwallader said, "to be without fear of dying. To be indestructible. Invincible. Not to have to worry about disease. Accidents. Pestilence. War. Famine. Anything. Governments and institutions disintegrate. People die. But Walter Bedeker goes on and on!"

Bedeker, his head tilted, a smile playing on his puckish, gnome-like face, walked over to the mirror and studied his reflection. "Walter Bedeker goes on and on," he said thoughtfully.

Mr. Cadwallader stepped up behind him so that his reflection joined Bedeker's.

"Mr. Cadwallader," Bedeker said, "about this soul. You say I won't miss it?"

"Why, you'll never know it's gone."

"And I'll go on and on quite unable to die, you say?"
"Quite."

"No tricks?" Bedeker asked. "No hidden clauses? I'll just live as long as I want to live, is that it?"

Cadwallader chuckled at him. "That's it. That's precisely it."

Mr. Cadwallader went back over to his chair and sat

down again. Bedeker remained at the mirror studying his face, running a questioning finger over it.

"How about my appearance?" he asked.

"I'm afraid I can't do much about that," Cadwallader said thoughtlessly, but he glided over the slip. "What I mean is—you should look pretty much the same."

"But in five hundred years," Bedeker insisted, "I don't want to look like any dried up old prune."

Cadwallader looked up toward the ceiling, and shook his head at the enormity of the competition. "Oh, Mr. Bedeker," he said, "you drive a mean bargain. A most difficult bargain. But," he made a gesture of resignation, "you'll find me a co-operative"—he smiled apologetically while he searched for the right word—"man?—And we'll throw this into the bargain. Whatever aging takes place on your features will be more or less imperceptible."

Bedeker turned to him from the mirror. "Cadwallader, I believe we're close to making a deal."

Cadwallader began to rub his hands together and then quickly put them behind his back. "Mr. Bedeker," he said happily, "you'll never regret this. Not to your dying day!"

Bedeker looked at him sharply. "Which by rights," Cadwallader added hurriedly, "should not be for several thousand years. However, there is something, Mr. Bedeker—"

Bedeker waggled a finger at him. "Ah ha. Ah ha. Ah ha! Now it comes out, huh?"

"It's for your benefit, I can assure you." Cadwallader took a large, thick document from his pocket and thumbed through it. "Article 93," he exclaimed. "Here it is, right here." He pointed to the page and turned it around so that Bedeker could see it.

"What about it?" Bedeker asked warily. "Read it to me."

The fat gentleman cleared his throat. "It's in the nature of an escape clause," he said. "*Your* escape clause. Whereas the party of the first part upon due notification to the party of the second part—" Cadwallader mumbled. "Oh, this is tiresome. I'll just give it to you thumb nail. It's simply this. If you ever get tired of living, Mr.

Bedeker, you can exercise this clause by calling on me and requesting your—" He smiled. "Oh there go the semantics again. Your demise? At which point I shall see to it that you are given a rapid and uncomplicated—" he held up his hands and wiggled his fat fingers—"departure?"

Bedeker puckered up his mouth in a wise, elfish little look, snapped his fingers and beckoned for the document. Cadwallader handed it over with a flourish, then loosened his tie as Bedeker riffled through the pages. Mr. Cadwallader took a large crimson handkerchief from his hip pocket and wiped his face.

"You sure keep it hot in here!" he murmured.

Bedeker finished the last page, then handed the document back to the fat man.

"It appears to be in order, Mr. Cadwallader, but I can assure you that I'm not the sort of man to kill the goose that lays the golden egg. When you talk immortality to me, brother, I *mean* immortality! You're going to have a long, long, long wait!"

Again Cadwallader bowed his assent. "Mr. Bedeker," he said, "Nothing would please me more!"

Bedeker said, "Then I think you've got a deal."

This time Mr. Cadwallader couldn't restrain himself from rubbing his hands together. His eyes positively glittered and it struck Bedeker that he was looking at a two-holed opening into a furnace. He could reflect no longer upon this because Mr. Cadwallader reached into the air and pulled out what appeared to be a smoking rubber stamp. This he swung in a wide arc and brought it down on the front page of the document. There was a sizzling sound and the document floated to the floor, burning at the edge. Bedeker could see that on the lower right-hand corner was the imprint of a seal. It looked like a circle with horns in the middle. After a moment the fire went out and the paper lay smoking. Bedeker bent over and picked it up.

"Yes, it seems to be pretty much in order," Bedeker said. "Now a few other questions, Mr.—"

But the room was empty. He thought he heard the sound of distant laughter retreating into the night, but he wasn't sure and soon he heard nothing. Bedeker carefully folded the document and shoved it in the dresser drawer. He smiled at himself in the mirror, then went to the window and with an impulsive gesture, he flung it open, letting the cold air rush into the room. He stood beating his chest and breathing deeply. He had never in his life felt so free, so unencumbered, and so absolutely healthy.

This reminded Bedeker of his tray, with all its medicines, bottles, jars, lotions, and his book, *How To Be Happy Though Bedridden*. He picked them up and hurled them out the window, smiling as after a few seconds, he heard the bottles smash on the pavement fourteen stories below. Turning from the window, he noticed the hot water pipes. A shimmering heat rose from them and they looked brick red in the lamp light. He approached them gingerly, and stood over them, very slowly raising his hands until he could feel the heat pour into his palms and through his fingers. Red hot, he noted. *Red hot.*

"Proof of the pudding," Bedeker murmured, "And no time like the present!"

He slammed both palms down on the pipes, listened to the sizzle of the burning flesh, watched the smoke rise in front of his eyes. But there was no sensation of pain. There was no sensation of any kind. He lifted his hands and stared at them. Not a mark. He looked down at the red hot pipes, and laughed aloud. He continued to laugh, his head back, as he walked across the room and threw himself on the bed. He heard the bedroom door open and Ethel stood there staring at him, frightened.

"Walter," she said nervously. "Is everything all right?"

"Is everything all right?" he repeated. "Everything, Ethel, my love, is delightful. Everything is superb. Everything is perfect."

He got up and went to the dresser. There was a nail file lying alongside a brush set. He picked it up and smiling happily, jammed the point into his palm. Ethel screamed and fell back against the door. Then very slowly she opened her eyes to look at the Cheshire-cat grin on her husband's face. He held out an unscathed palm.

"See, my dear? The hand is quicker than the eye! The

proof of the pudding! Witness, my dear . . . the new Walter Bedeker!"

He started to laugh again, a gusty, roaring, uncontrollable laugh and he paraded back and forth across the room like a rooster in a barnyard. Ethel stood still, her face pale, wondering if she dared leave the room to get to the telephone. Or if at any moment the demented man in front of her might get violent. Her eye fell on the nail file on the dresser. She gasped, bit deep into a knuckle, and looked at Walter in horror. There had been blood on the nail file.

In the weeks that followed, Ethel Bedeker was never sure whether or not she preferred the old days to these new ones. Or whether perhaps it had been an irreparable mistake to have been married or even born. The "new" Walter Bedeker turned out to be a mystifying individual. True, he no longer betook himself to his bed five times a month and screamed impossible demands. As a matter of fact, he was rarely home any more. But his new behavior was equally disturbing.

The first indication she got of what might be expected was a phone call from an insurance adjuster attached to a building firm. Walter, it seemed, had been hit by a falling steel "I" beam that weighed about two and a half tons. It had been in the process of being raised by a chain to the tenth floor of an office building under construction. The chain had broken and the beam had fallen three hundred feet to land on Walter's head and smash him down into the sidewalk. The foreman on the job first had been violently ill, then had walked very slowly toward that spot in the sidewalk where the horror was waiting for him. He covered his eyes because of a normal reluctance to view mangled bodies. He had also peeked between two fingers, because of the equally normal trait of being fascinated by the horrible. He was to be disappointed on both scores, because Walter Bedeker had crawled out from underneath the beam, none the worse for being squashed, except that his clothes were ripped and his hair disheveled. He had thundered at the foreman that he'd better contact his lawyer because there was going to be one helluva whopping suit in the offing.

It was to tell Ethel all this that the insurance adjuster had phoned, and to inform her that he was on his way to their apartment.

That afternoon Walter signed a waiver of further claim and collected a check for five thousand dollars.

This happened on a Wednesday and the following Saturday afternoon Walter was alone in the self-service elevator when for some strange reason the main cable broke, and the elevator car shot down the two-thousand-foot shaft to be smashed to smithereens at the bottom. The building superintendent heard his shrieking voice echoing up through the shaft and went down to the basement to pry open the wrecked door. Bedeker lay in the rubble with nothing injured, not even his aplomb. (This affair was settled for thirty-eight hundred dollars and forty-two cents.)

A week later Bedeker was standing in front of a fireworks factory when the building went up in smoke. The newspapers called it the worst fire disaster to occur in the city in twenty-five years. Luckily, it happened after the five o'clock whistle, and only three bodies were found, burnt beyond recognition, in the debris. Bedeker had been buried under a collapsing, burning wall, but had crawled out on his hands and knees right to the foot of a fireman who had fainted dead away upon seeing him. His clothes had been burnt entirely off his body and this accounted for the figure of thirty-nine dollars and fifty cents added to the ten thousand for which the fireworks company settled with him.

In the next five weeks Bedeker was in eight major accidents—a subway collision, a bus over-turning, five automobile accidents (in each case the driver swore that Bedeker had stepped out in front of the speeding car), and a decidedly freakish circumstance in a restaurant where Bedeker complained there was glass in his beef stew. It wasn't until after the manager had paid Bedeker two hundred dollars in cash that the waiter showed the manager a half-chewed glass on the table. By this time

Bedeker had walked out in a huff, pocketing his two hundred dollars and was no more to be seen.

It was now New Year's Eve and Ethel had timidly asked Bedeker if they could go out to dinner or to a show or perhaps to a nightclub. Bedeker stood at the window, his back to her, not answering.

"Eleven accidents," he said, "that's what I've been in. Eleven accidents."

Ethel, who had just mentioned that it was a long time since they'd been dancing together, tried another tack.

"That's the point, dear," she said hopefully. "You need recreation. You need to get your mind off things."

Bedeker continued to stare out the window. "Wouldn't you think, Ethel," he asked rhetorically, "that there'd be an element of thrill in eleven accidents? Eleven accidents in which you *know* nothing can happen to you?"

"I guess so, Walter," Ethel answered irresolutely, not understanding a thing he was talking about.

"Well, it's a fact," Bedecker continued. "There should be an excitement in this sort of thing." He walked away from the window. *"Well, there isn't.* It's dull. It's absolutely without the remotest bit of excitement. In short, I'm bored with it."

"Walter, dear," Ethel said softly, "I guess we should count our blessings."

"You, Ethel," Bedeker snapped, "should shut your mouth. You look for all the world like a small gray mouse searching for a piece of cheese."

She let the cold, hurt feeling subside before she answered him.

"Walter, you can be terribly cruel, do you know that?"

Bedeker rolled his eyes upward and said, "Ethel, please shut your mouth!" He paced the room back and forth. "I swear he cheated me! Mortal-shmortal! What's the good of it when there aren't any kicks? Any excitement at all!"

Ethel found herself looking at him in helpless confusion. He was Walter Bedeker all right. He was her husband. But he was totally and distinctly different from the man she married, the hypochondriac she had lived with for so many years.

"Walter," she asked, "do you feel all right?"

Bedeker ignored her. "At least when I was concerned about my health," he said aloud to no one, "there was an element of risk there. But now there is no risk. There is no excitement. There is no nothing!"

He suddenly cocked his head slightly, his eyes grew wide and he ran past her to the bathroom. She heard him fumbling through the medicine chest over the sink. There was the clatter of bottles and of glass.

"Ethel?" he called from the bathroom. "Do we have any starch?"

Ethel walked toward the bathroom door. "Starch?" she asked.

Bedeker said, "Of course, starch."

Ethel looked over his shoulder at the bottles he had lined up. There was iodine, rubbing alcohol and epsom salts. He had one glass into which he was pouring sizable portions from each.

"Starch!" Bedeker repeatedly impatiently.

Ethel went to the kitchen and got a bottle of starch from a cabinet under the sink. She brought it to Bedeker and he immediately unscrewed the top and poured this last ingredient into the mixture, which foamed and took on a kind of mustard color. Bedeker held up the glass, and with a quick motion, drank it all down. Ethel gaped at him as he smacked his lips, looked at his face in the mirror, stuck out his tongue, then put the glass down disconsolately.

"You see?" he asked.

"See what?" Her voice trembled.

"See what I just drank? Iodine, rubbing alcohol, epsom salts and starch. And what did it do to me, Ethel? I ask you—what did it do to me? It did nothing! Absolutely nothing. I've just drunk enough poison to kill a dozen men and it tasted like lemonade. *Weak* lemonade."

Ethel leaned against the door. Her voice was very steady. "Walter," she said, "I want to know what this is all about!"

Bedeker peered at her elfishly. "What it's all about? You really want to know?"

She nodded.

"All right," Bedeker said, "I'll tell you. I happen to be immortal. I am indestructible. I made a pact with a man named Cadwallader who has given me immortality in exchange for my soul. More succinctly than that, I couldn't put it."

Ethel caught a brief look at her reflection in the mirror and wondered in part of her brain how any woman could look so pale and so frightened.

"I want you to sit down, Walter," she said, collecting herself. "I'm going to make you some tea and then I'm going to call the doctor."

She turned to leave and Bedeker grabbed her arm, yanking her around to face him.

"You will *not* make tea," he commanded. "And you will *not* call the doctor. If you had any imagination at all, Ethel, you *might* tell me what I could do to get a little excitement out of all of this. I've been in subway crashes, bus accidents, major fires and just now I drank poison. You *saw* me." He paused and shrugged. "Nothing! Absolutely nothing. You know what I've been thinking?" He left the bathroom and walked back into the living room. "I have been thinking, Ethel, that I should go up to the roof and throw myself down the light well! Smack dab down the light well. Fourteen stories down just for the experience of it."

Ethel sat heavily down in a chair, close to tears now. "Please, Walter. Please, for goodness sake—"

Bedeker went toward the door. "Ethel, darling, shut your mouth."

She sprang to her feet and raced to the door, intercepting him just as he started to open it.

"Walter," she beseeched him. "Please, Walter, for God's sake—"

He pushed her out of the way and went out, down the hall, to the rear stairs and started to climb. Ethel followed him, pleading all the way, arguing, cajoling, but he would have none of it. On the roof, he headed toward the light well. It was a big, square hole covered by glass. There was a small concrete shelf around it that stood only about eight inches high. Ethel immediately got between Walter and the concrete strip, and held out her hands to him.

"Please, Walter," she said. "Please, my darling——"

Bedeker said, "Ethel, go drown in the tub and leave me alone. I'm going head first down that light well, and I want you to get out of the way!"

He advanced toward her and she backed away from him.

"Please, darling," she said. "Please come back to the apartment. I'll make you potato pancakes. Remember, you used to love potato pancakes."

Bedeker yanked her arm away from him, pushed her aside. "You, my dear," he said, "are a potato pancake. You look like a potato pancake. You have all the excitement of a potato pancake. You are as tasteless as a potato pancake. Now I've told you for the last time to get out of my way."

She threw herself against him, struggling to push him back and only at the last instant did she realize that her foot was no longer on the level of the roof floor. It dangled over the concrete stoop surrounding the stairwell. In a moment her balance shifted and she had fallen backwards, smashing through the glass, and hurtled fourteen stories down to the concrete courtyard below. Even her scream was a quiet, pathetic noise coming from a quiet, pathetic woman. It was more misery than horror; more a gentle protest than the last utterance of a woman going head first to her death.

Bedeker tiptoed over to the light well and looked down. Lights were going on sporadically on every other floor like the panel board of an elevator announcing the stops. He scratched his jaw, took out a cigarette and lit it.

"I wonder what it felt like," he said softly.

Some place off in the distance he heard a siren. There was a growing mumble and jumble of voices inside the building. Then suddenly he had a thought. It was a wonderful thought. An exciting thought. He hurried to the door leading to the rear stairs, went down them two at a time, trotted into his apartment and picked up the telephone.

"Operator," he said, "get me the police, please. Immediately. It's an emergency." After a moment he heard the voice of a desk sergeant at the local precinct. "Hello? Is this the police station? Well, this is Walter Bedeker, 11 North 7th Street. That's correct. Apartment 12B. Will you please come over here right away. No, no trouble. I just killed my wife. That's right. Yes, I'll stay right here. Good-by."

He put the receiver down, took a deep luxurious drag on his cigarette, flicked the ashes away and said, "Well, let's give the old electric chair a whirl!"

The trial of the State vs. Walter Bedeker was, in the words of the District Attorney "the most predictable thing to hit town since professional wrestling." The court reporters, spectators, and certainly the jury seemed to share the prosecution's view. In three days of proceedings, the State made one telling point after the other. They established motive. (Six witnesses had testified to the fights between Walter Bedeker and his wife.) They showed premeditation. (The janitor testified that he had heard Bedeker threaten his wife on at least a dozen occasions.) And they did everything but bring in photographs of the actual commission of crime. (At least ten neighbors had seen Bedeker come down off the roof and hurry back into his apartment.)

So in short, Mr. Walter Bedeker sat alongside of his lawyer on the eve of the last day of trial in a most vulnerable position. You could not have told this, however, by looking at Walter Bedeker. He sat half smiling at the judge, the witnesses, the prosecution. On the stand he openly and freely admitted he had pushed his wife down the light well and had no misgivings about it at all. As a matter of fact, he would do it again.

His lawyer, hired by the State, was a desperately energetic young man who objected on the slightest provocation, who argued, pleaded and thundered throughout the trial, who parried every telling thrust on the part of the prosecution and parried well. But his was a losing cause and he knew it. He became acutely aware of just how losing it was when after sending a penciled note of inquiry over to his client he received the note back with the following scrawl underneath his question: "Go to hell, affectionately, Walter Bedeker." From that point on the defense was reasonably certain that the normal rapport between client and lawyer did not exist in this case. And further, that this was a client whose answers on the stand seemed to suggest collusion between him and the prosecution. Because Walter Bedeker was convicting himself with every answer, every gesture, obviously because he wished to.

On the evening of the third day of trial, Bedeker's lawyer went to see Bedeker in his cell. He arrived during his client's dinner and found himself completely ignored until Bedeker had started his dessert. Then the little man looked up as if suddenly realizing the lawyer was there and nodded perfunctorily.

"Cooper, the legal beagle. What brings you here at this odd hour?"

Cooper sat down on the other chair and studied his client. "Mr. Bedeker," he said grimly, "you may not realize this, but at the rate things are going this case will go to the jury by tomorrow."

Bedeker nodded and continued to spoon down ice cream. "How do you feel, Cooper?" he asked.

Cooper squirmed with frustration and put his brief case on the floor. "How am I? I'm miserable, Mr. Bedeker. I've been miserable since I took your case. I've had tough clients before, but nobody like you."

"Really?" Bedeker asked insouciantly. "What disturbs you?"

"What disturbs me is that in three days of trial you've acted like a man desperate to get convicted. When I examine you, you shut up like a clam. When the prosecuting attorney examines you, you act as if you were betting on him to win the case." He leaned forward intensely. "Now look, Bedeker, this is the goods here. If this case goes to the jury tomorrow as things stand now, you don't have chance number one."

Bedeker lit a cigarette and leaned back on his cot. "Is that a fact?" he asked.

"That is a fact. Now tomorrow this is what I want us to do!"

He lifted the brief case and unzipped it. He was diving into it for papers when Bedeker said, "Don't bother, Mr. Cooper. Just don't bother." He waved at the brief case. "Put it away."

"How's that?" Cooper asked.

"Put it away."

Cooper stared at him for a long, unbelieving moment. "Bedeker, did you get what I was trying to tell you? You're about twelve hours away from a guilty verdict on a charge of first degree murder."

Bedeker smiled and clucked. "And what will the penalty be?"

"The penalty," Cooper said tiredly, "in this State for first degree murder is death in the electric chair."

"Death in the electric chair," Bedeker repeated. He tapped his fingers on the side of the cot and then examined his nails.

"Bedeker," Cooper shouted, almost beyond control.

"Death in the electric chair. And if I were in California?"

"What?" Cooper asked incredulously.

"How would they try to kill me if I lived in California," Bedeker said.

"Capital punishment there is the gas chamber, but I frankly don't see why—"

"And in Kansas?" Bedeker interrupted.

"In Kansas," Cooper answered, "it's hanging. Now I'm going to tell you something, Bedeker—"

Bedeker rose from the cot and surveyed the lawyer who now had a thin covering of perspiration over his face.

"No, Mr. Cooper," Bedeker said mildly. "I'm going to tell *you* something. The only thing they'll get for their trouble if they try to electrocute me is a whopping electricity bill! Now good night, Mr. Cooper. See you in court!"

Cooper sighed deeply. He slowly zipped up his brief case and rose. "I don't know, Bedeker," he said. "I just don't understand you. The alienist says you're sane and you say you killed your wife. But way down deep I know you didn't. So tomorrow when I sum up for you,

I'm going to lead from terrible weakness." He shrugged hopelessly. "But I intend to do the best I can."

He turned and went to the cell door, tapping on it for the guard. After a moment they heard him coming down the corridor. He unlocked the door and Cooper walked out.

"Mr. Cooper," Bedeker's voice came from behind the bars.

The defense attorney turned to look at him.

Bedeker smiled at him. "Mr. Cooper," he said. "Really—don't bother!"

The prosecution on the following morning delivered one of the briefest summations in a murder trial ever presented in the history of the State. It lasted only a minute and a half and afterwards the District Attorney walked smiling and confident back to his seat. Mr. Cooper rose for his summation and after about ten seconds of a stumbling if sincere start, he seemed to warm up and a relatively listless jury suddenly seemed very aware of him. Even the judge leaned over on his elbows to listen more intently. A court reporter later described it as one helluva summation—one of the best ever heard in that courtroom.

"Guilty, yes," Cooper roared. "But premeditated? Hardly!" His client, Cooper contended, had *not* led his wife up to the roof. She had followed him. No witness had proven otherwise. Killed her—yes, this he did. Pushed her off the stoop, down the light well—absolutely. No contest. But had he planned to do it? This was a moot point. Twenty-eight minutes later after an address loaded with moot points, Cooper sat down next to Walter Bedeker and listened to the murmur run through the courtroom. Bedeker smiled vaguely at him. He hadn't been listening. He was busy jotting notes on a pad. Things he intended to do after he got out. Cooper could see a few of his scrawled plans over Bedeker's shoulder. "Land on third rail in subway station." "Jump in front of diesel engine." "Hide in hydrogen bomb testing area." Etc. Etc.

Sixty-three minutes later the jury came back with a verdict of guilty and shortly thereafter Walter Bedeker stood in front of the bench for his sentencing. He leaned against the bench on his elbow, picked his teeth, yawned and looked generally bored. Walter Bedeker had paid little heed to the proceedings in that courtroom. Even now he scarcely heard what the judge was saying. Something to the effect that the court prescribed life imprisonment. It was not the words that jarred him. Rather it was Cooper, grabbing him, hugging him, shaking him.

"Life imprisonment, old man," Cooper screamed into his ear joyfully. "I knew we could do it! I just knew we could do it."

As the turnkey led Bedeker through the side door of the courtroom he became gradually aware of the hum of voices around him. "God, what a summation!" "Life imprisonment—masterful!" "There's one helluva lucky man!"

It wasn't until Bedeker was walking down the corridor outside that he realized what had happened. Cooper had got him off with life imprisonment. He stopped, turned toward the courtroom at the other end of the corridor and screamed out loud, "Wait a minute! *WAIT A MINUTE!* I can't get imprisoned for life! Don't they understand? Don't they know what this means? *I can't go to prison for life."*

He began to cry. He was crying when they put him in the black paddy wagon to take him back to jail. He cried all during the trip and that night in his cell he was still crying.

When the cell guard brought him his dinner he noted that Mr. Bedeker's eyes were red-rimmed and that he only toyed with his food.

"You're a lucky guy, Bedeker," the guard said through the cell doors. "Tomorrow they'll be taking you to the penitentiary. That'll be your new home. It's a long way from the death cell."

Bedeker didn't answer. He sat looking down at the tray of food on his lap and felt the rising bubbles of sadness and hopelessness and misery crawl up his body and he had to stifle a sob.

"Look at it this way," the guard said philosophically. "What's life, Mr. Bedeker? Forty years. Fifty years. Hell, you can do that standing on your head." Bedeker could hear him as he went down the corridor. "That's all. Forty, fifty years. Maybe not even that much—"

Bedeker set the tray on the floor and put his head in his hands.

"Forty, fifty years," he murmured to himself. "Forty or fifty years. Or sixty, or seventy, or a hundred, or two hundred."

Numbers drifted across the mind. Five figure numbers. Six figure numbers. And he heard a voice thundering at him from no place in particular.

"After all, what are a few hundred years or a few thousand? Or five thousand or ten thousand? What is it in the scheme of things?" The voice ended on a note of laughter. Big laughter. Resounding, quaking laughter that came from the belly of a fat man.

Walter Bedeker looked up to see the corpulent blue-suited figure of Cadwallader standing in the middle of the cell grinning at him, his white teeth gleaming, his eyes suddenly coal-red.

"Mr. Bedeker," he rumbled. "Just think of it! Immortality . . . indestructibility . . . institutions fail, governments disintegrate, people die! But Walter Bedeker goes on and on." His laugh was rolling thunder across the cell. "Walter Bedeker goes on and on. And on and on and on."

Bedeker screamed and buried his face against the pillow on the cot. There was an odor in the cell. A burning odor. Was it brimstone? Very likely.

"Mr. Bedeker?" Cadwallader's voice was soft now, the words arrived on velvet. "About that escape clause. Would you care to exercise it now?"

Bedeker never even raised his head from the pillow. He nodded and a moment thereafter felt a pain sear across his chest, a terrible pain. A pain more agonizing than anything he'd ever felt before. His body twitched convulsively and he fell off the cot to land on his back, his eyes staring lifelessly up toward the cell. Walter Bedeker was a dead body. The thing that had been his soul let out a strangled scream and struggled inside the pocket of a blue suit as it was carried into another dimension.

The guard found Walter Bedeker during bed check that night. He opened the cell door, rushed in and felt for a pulse. Then he'd called the prison doctor and the warden. It was a heart attack and this was written on a cardboard tag that was attached to his chart.

A comment was made by one of the attendants in the prison morgue. It was something to the effect that he'd never seen a look of such utter horror on a man's face as that which Walter Bedeker's wore as they shoved him into a refrigerated compartment and closed the door.

From Rod Serling's closing narration, "Escape Clause," The Twilight Zone, November 6, 1959, CBS Television Network.

The CAMERA PANS away from the body and then slowly up the side of the cell until it stops on a shot of the barred window facing the outside.

> NARRATOR'S VOICE
> There's a saying . . . every man is put
> on earth condemned to die. Time and
> method of execution unknown.
>   (a pause)
> Perhaps this is as it should be. Case
> in point—Walter Bedeker, lately
> deceased. A little man with such a
> yen to live.

Now the CAMERA MOVES OUT and through the bars and is shooting up into the night sky.

> NARRATOR'S VOICE
> Beaten by the devil . . . by his own boredom . . .
> and by the scheme of things in this . . .
> the Twilight Zone.
>   FADE TO BLACK

Walking Distance

His name was Martin Sloan and he was thirty-six years old. As he looked at his reflection in the dresser mirror, he felt that recurring surprise that the tall, attractive man staring back was he, and beyond that was the wonder that the image bore no real relationship to the man himself. There was Martin Sloan, a tall six-foot-two with a lean, suntanned face, a straight nose and a square jaw; just a few threads of gray on either temple, medium-set eyes—a good face, all in all. The inventory continued down the glass. Brooks Brothers suit that fitted with casual perfection, Hathaway shirt and silk tie, thin gold watch, and all of it so appropriate, so full of taste.

He continued to stare at himself and marveled at how a veneer could be spread over a man's frame to camouflage what was underneath. Because that's what he was looking at at this moment—camouflage. Hell, yes, he was Martin Sloan, an ad agency exec, with a fabulous bachelor apartment on Park overlooking Sixty-Third, and he drove a red Mercedes-Benz and he was an agile-minded, very creative, oh, so subtly pushy kind of rising young man. He could order in French and call Jackie Gleason by his first name and feel the very odd warmth of status when the maitre d' at Sardi's East, or the Colony, or Danny's Hideway, called him by name, and smiled a quiet, respectful deference when he entered their places.

But the hell of it, the misery of it was that Martin Sloan had an incipient ulcer that at this moment began a slow, raking crawl over his insides. He knew panic a dozen times a day—that convulsive, breath-stopping, ice-cube feeling of doubt and indecision; of being second guessed, of being wrong; the effort to make his voice firm, his decisions sound irrevocable, when deep inside his gut—worse as each day passed—he felt a vague slipping away of all the props he conjured up and took on the stage with him when he faced the president of the agency, the clients, or the other account execs.

And that ulcer! That God-damned ulcer. He felt it rise in him again and tensed himself like a man going into a cold shower. It burned across his stomach. After it subsided, he lit a cigarette and felt the wetness on his back as the hot June perspiration turned his Hathaway shirt into a clinging, itchy thing and made his palms sodden extensions of himself.

Martin Sloan went to the window to look out at New York. The lights were on along Park Avenue and he remembered the lights of his home town. He often thought about his home town lately. For the past several months he had been coming back to the apartment from the office to sit in the dark living room and drink long, solitary scotches; to think about himself as a boy, and where it had all begun—the chronology of the thirty-six year old man who had the world by the short hair, but at least three times a week felt like crying.

Sloan gazed down at the Park Avenue lights and thought about himself as a boy and the main street of his town and the drugstore that Mr. Wilson owned. Sporadic, unrelated remembrances, but part of a bittersweet pattern that made that room, the scotch, the reflection in the mirror so unbearable. Again he felt that urge to cry and pushed it down deep inside of him along with the pain of the ulcer. A thought came to him. Get in the car and go. Get out of New York. Away from Madison Avenue. Away from the blathering, meaningless, mixed-metaphored jargon of his boss; the ratings and the "percentages-of-audience" and the cosmetic accounts and the three-million-dollar gross billings and that sick, ugly façade of good fellowship among strangers.

Some kind of ghostly billy club tapped at his ankles and told him it was later than he thought. He left his apartment, picked 'up his car, drove out on to Grand Central Parkway. Hunched over the wheel of his red Mercedes-Benz he asked himself very briefly just where the hell did he think he was going and he was undismayed by the fact that there wasn't an answer. He wanted to think, that was all. He wanted to remember. And when he turned off on the New York Throughway and headed upstate he had no further resolves. He just kept driving on into the night and was only dimly aware that old man Wilson's drugstore seemed strangely etched in his mind. It was this picture that sent his brain back on an errand to recapture memories of a time before. Memories of a place called Homewood, New York, a quiet, tree-filled little town of three thousand people. As he drove, he remembered what had been a minute fragment of his life, but God what a fragment! The wondrous time of growing up. Quiet streets on a summer night. The joy of parks and playgrounds. The uninhibited freedom of a child. Memories ebbed back and forth across his mind and left him with a strange, indefinable hunger that subconsciously he realized was not just for a place—but for a time. He wanted to be a boy again. That was what he wanted. He wanted to turn around in his life and go backwards. He wanted to run past the years to find the one in which he was eleven years old.

Martin Sloan, in a Brooks Brothers suit, driving a red sports car, headed out into the night and away from New York. He drove with an urgency and a purpose without really knowing his destination. This was no week-end drive. It was no momentary turning of his back to convention, and habit. This was an exodus. This was flight. Somewhere at the end of a long, six-lane highway that stretched out across the rolling hills of upstate New York, Martin Sloan was looking for sanity.

He stopped at a motel near Binghamton, New York,

slept a few hours, and was on his way again, and at nine in the morning pulled into a gas station off the State highway. He'd been going fast and the car squealed to a stop sending up clouds of dust. A little of the drive that sustained him in New York, a little of the impatience that pushed him through the days, clung to him now and he honked the horn persistently. The attendant, a nice-looking kid in dungarees looked up from the tire he was repairing a few yards away, wiped his hands with a cloth and stood listening to Martin Sloan's horn.

"How about some service?" Martin yelled.

"How about some quiet?" the attendant answered him.

Martin bit his lower lip and turned away, gripping the steering wheel, studying the dashboard.

"I'm sorry," he said softly.

The attendant came toward him.

"Would you fill it up, please?" Martin asked.

"Sure."

"I said I was sorry," Martin said.

"I heard you," the attendant answered. "You take high-test in these things, don't you?"

Martin nodded, handed him the keys to the gas tank. The attendant went around to the rear of the car and unlocked the tank.

"How about an oil change and a lube job, too?" Martin asked him.

"Sure," the attendant said. "It'll take about an hour."

Martin said, "I've got plenty of time."

He turned to look across the road at a sign which read, "Homewood, 1 1/2 miles."

"That's Homewood up ahead, isn't it?" Martin asked.

The attendant said, "Yep."

"I used to live there. Grew up there as a matter of fact. I haven't been back in eighteen . . . twenty years."

He got out of the car, reached in his pocket for a cigarette and noticed that it was his last one. There was a cigarette machine in front of the station. Martin got a pack of cigarettes from it and came back, still talking.

"Eighteen . . . twenty years. And then last night I—I just got in the car and drove. Reached a point where I, well—I had to get out of New York. One more board meeting, phone call, report, problem—" He laughed and the laugh sounded hollow and tired.

"New York, is that where you're from?" the attendant asked.

"That's right. New York."

"I see you guys all the time," the attendant said. "Take a drive in the country—gotta go a hundred miles an hour. Stop for a red light, somebody beats you startin' up when she turns green, then your day's ruined. God, how do you guys keep at it?"

Martin turned away and fiddled with the side mirror on his car. "We just do," he answered. "We just keep at it and then there comes a June night—when we suddenly take off." He looked across the road again toward the sign. "A mile and a half," he mused. "That's walking distance."

"For some people," the attendant answered him.

Martin grinned. "But not for New York executives in red sports cars, huh?"

The attendant shrugged.

"I'll come back for the car later on." Martin grinned. "A mile and a half—that's walking distance!"

He took off his coat and slung it over his shoulder and tramped down the road to Homewood, a little over a mile away—and twenty years later.

Martin entered the drugstore and stood motionless near the door in the dark coolness. It was exactly as he remembered it. A narrow, high-ceilinged room with an old-fashioned soda bar on one side, a counter on the other. A wooden stairway that led to a small office off a tiny balcony. This was where Mr. Wilson, the owner, used to take his catnaps, Martin remembered. A thin little man with thick glasses wiped soda glasses and smiled at Martin across the fountain.

"What'll it be?" he asked.

Martin looked at the posters on the walls, the old-fashioned hanging lights, the two big electric fans that hung down from the ceiling. He went to the counter and sat down. The five big glass jars of penny candy were just as he remembered them.

"You still make great chocolate sodas?" he asked the man behind the soda bar. "Three scoops?"

The man's smile looked a little strained. "How's that?"

Martin's laugh was apologetic. "I used to spend half my life in this drugstore," he explained. "I grew up here. The one thing I always remember ordering—that was a chocolate ice cream soda with three scoops. And it was ten cents, too."

The little man looked at him quizzically and Martin studied his face.

"You know," Martin said, "you look familiar to me. Have I seen you before?"

The clerk shrugged and grinned. "I got that kind of a face."

"It's been a long time," Martin said. "Eighteen . . . twenty years. That's when I left." Then he laughed at a collection of secret thoughts that crossed his mind. "I wish I had a buck," he continued, "for every hour I spent at this fountain though. From grammar school right through third-year high." He turned on the stool to look out at the bright, sunny street outside. "Town looks the same too." He turned back to the little man. "You know it's really amazing. After twenty years to look so exactly the same."

The little man in glasses fixed his soda and then handed it to him. "That'll be a dime."

Martin started to fish in his pocket, then stopped abruptly. "A dime?" he asked incredulously. He held up the giant, richly dark glass. "Three scoops?"

The soda jerk laughed. "That's the way we make 'em."

Martin laughed again. "You're going to lose your shirt. Nobody sells sodas for a dime any more."

There was a moment's silence then the little man asked, "They don't? Where *you* from?"

Martin started to spoon down some of the chocolate ice cream. "New York," he said between gulps. "Hey, you make a great soda!"

The little man leaned on the counter with his elbows. "Taste okay?" he asked.

"Wonderful." He finished the ice cream and slurped up the last of the soda water. He grinned. "Like I never left home. That was great." He turned to scan the room. "Funny," he said, "how many memories you connect with a place. I always thought if I ever came back here, it'd all be changed."

The store looked back at him. The counters and shelves and posters and lights. The electric fans. They looked back at him like old friends. "It's just as if—" Martin said thoughtfully, "—as if I'd left yesterday." He got off the stool and stood twirling it. "Just as if I'd been away overnight." He smiled at the soda jerk. "I'd almost expect Mr. Wilson to be sitting up there in the office and sleeping away his afternoons just the way he always did before he died."

He didn't see the soda jerk start at this.

"That's one of the images I have," he continued. "Old Man Wilson sleeping in his big comfortable chair in his office up there. Old Man Wilson—may his soul rest in peace."

He reached in his pocket, took out a dollar bill and put it on the counter. The soda jerk stared at it, surprised.

"That's a buck!"

Martin smiled at him, tapped the glass with a finger. "That—" he looked around the room— "and all of this, they're worth it."

He went back out into the hot summer. The soda jerk leaned on the counter, wondering about Martin, then lifted up the top of the chocolate syrup container and peered inside. He replaced it, came around from behind the counter, climbed the stairs, and tapped gently on a door. A muffled, sleepy voice, responded.

"Yes?"

The soda jerk opened the door a few inches. "Mr. Wilson," he said to the white-haired old man, sitting in the heavy leather chair, one eye open, "We need more chocolate syrup."

The old man winked, nodded and closed his eyes again. "I'll order some this afternoon."

In a moment he was fast asleep again. The soda jerk went back to the counter. He took Martin Sloan's glass and started to wash it. Funny guy, he thought. Lose

your shirt if you sell three scoops for a dime. He chuckled as he was drying the glass. Nobody sold three scoops
for a dime any more. Then he shrugged and put the
glass away. You met all kinds. You sure met all kinds.
But this guy, this one was odd. This one had a look on his
face. How would you describe the look? He was so . . .
so *happy*. Just being in the dingy old drugstore, he looked
happy. A woman came in with a prescription and the soda
jerk didn't think of Martin Sloan any more that day.

Martin walked down Oak Street—the street he'd grown
up on. It stretched out ahead of him flanked by big, full-
leafed maple trees that cast sharp black shadows against
the brilliant whiteness of the sunshine. Big, two-story,
Victorian houses set back behind long, green lawns were
old friends to him. He rattled off names of their owners as
he walked slowly down the sidewalk. Vanburen. Wilcox.
Abernathy. He looked across the street. Over there, Dr.
Bradbury, Mulrooney, Grey. He stopped and leaned
against a tree. The street was exactly as he remembered
it. He felt the bittersweet pang of nostalgia. He remembered the games he'd played with the kids on this street.
The newspapers he'd delivered. The small-boy accidents
on roller skates and bicycles. And the people. The faces
and names that fused in his mind now. His house was on
the corner and for some reason he wanted to save this
for last. He could see it ahead of him. Big, white, with a
semi-circular porch running around it. Cupolas. An iron
jockey in front. God, the things you remembered. The
things you tucked away in an old mental trunk and
forgot. Then you opened the trunk and there they were.

"Hi," a little boy's voice said.

Martin Sloan looked down to see a four-year-old with
syrup on his face, shooting marbles. "Hi," Martin answered and sat down on the curb beside him. "You
pretty good?" He pointed toward the boy's marbles.

"At aggies?" the little boy said. "I'm not so bad."

Martin picked up one of the marbles and looked
through it. "I used to shoot marbles, too. We gave them
special names. The steel kind, the ballbearings we took
off old streetcars, we called them steelies. And the ones

we could see through—we called them clearies. Still call them names like that?"

"Sure," said the little boy.

Martin pointed across the street toward a telephone pole marked up by a thousand jackknives. "That's where we used to play hide-and-seek," he said to the boy. He grinned. "Draw a circle around the old man's back and who's to punch it." He laughed aloud as the thought warmed and delighted him. "Right on this street, every night in the summer we used to play that. And I used to live in that corner house down there," he pointed. "The big, white one."

"The Sloan house?" the little boy asked.

Martin's eyes grew a little wider. "That's right. You still call it that?"

"Still call it what?"

"The Sloan house. My name's Sloan. I'm Martin Sloan. What's your name?"

He held out his hand but the boy backed away, frowning at him.

"You're not Marty Sloan," the boy said accusingly. "I know Martin Sloan and you're not him."

Martin laughed. "I'm not, huh? Well, let's see what the driver's license says."

He reached into his breast pocket for his wallet. When he looked up the little boy was running down the street and then across a lawn to the house opposite his. Martin got slowly to his feet and began to walk again. It was the first slow walk, Martin reflected, that he'd taken in a long, long time. The houses and lawns went by and he drank them all in. He wanted this slow. He wanted to relish it all. In the distance he could hear children's laughter and the tinkle of an ice-cream wagon bell. It all fitted, sight and sound and mood. He got a tight feeling in his throat.

He didn't know how long he had walked but later he found himself in the park. Like the drugstore, like the houses, like the sounds—nothing had changed. There was the pavilion with the big, round, band-concert stand. There was the merry-go-round, loaded with kids, the brassy, discordant calliope music still chasing it round and round. There were the same wooden horses, the same brass rings, the same ice-cream stands, cotton candy-vendors. And always the children. Short pants and Mickey Mouse shirts. Lollipops and ice-cream cones and laughter and giggling. The language of the young. The music—the symphony of summer. The sounds swirled around him. Calliope, laughter, children. Again the tight feeling in his throat. Bittersweet again. All of it he had left so far behind and now he was so close to it.

A pretty young woman walked by him, wheeling a baby carriage. She stopped, caught by something she saw in Martin Sloan's face, as he watched the merry-go-round. She'd never seen a look quite like that before. It made her smile at him, and he smiled back.

"Wonderful place, isn't it?" he said.

"The park? It certainly is."

Martin nodded toward the merry-go-round. "That's a part of summer, isn't it? The music from the merry-go-round. The calliope."

The pretty woman laughed. "And the cotton candy and the ice cream and the band concert."

There was no smile on Martin's face now. It had been replaced by an intensity, a yearning. "There isn't anything quite as good ever," he said softly. "Not quite as good as summer and being a kid."

The woman stared at him. What was there about this man? "Are you from around here?" she asked.

Martin said, "A long time ago. I lived just a couple of blocks from here. I remember that bandstand. God, I should. I used to sneak away at night, lie over there on the grass staring up at the stars, listening to the music." His voice took on an excitement now. "I played ball on that field over there," he continued. "Third base. And I grew up with that merry-go-round." He pointed to the concert pavilion. "I carved my name on that post over there one summer. I was eleven years old and I carved my name right on—" He stopped abruptly and stared.

There was a small boy sitting on the railing of the pavilion carving something on the post with a jackknife. Martin Sloan walked slowly toward him. He felt a sensation he had never felt before. It was cold and heat and excitement. It was shock and surprise and a mystery he couldn't fathom. He looked up at the small boy and saw his own face of twenty-five years ago. He was looking at himself. He stood shaking his head from side to side, squinting up against the sun and then he saw what the boy was carving on the post. It was a kid's printed scrawl, the letters uneven. It read, "Martin Sloan." Martin caught his breath and pointed at the boy who was suddenly aware of him.

"Martin Sloan! *You're Martin Sloan.*"

The boy slid down from the railing. He looked frightened. "Yes, sir, but I didn't mean nothing, honest. Lots of kids carve their names here. Honest. I'm not the first one—"

Martin took a step closer to the boy. "You're Martin Sloan. Of course you're Martin Sloan, that's who you are. That's the way I looked."

He was unaware that his voice had suddenly become loud and of course he couldn't know how intense his face looked. The boy backed off and then scurried down the steps.

"Martin!" Sloan's voice followed him. "Martin, please —come back. Please, Martin."

He started to chase him and the boy disappeared in the multicolored crowd of shorts and Mickey Mouse shirts and mothers' cotton dresses.

"Please, Martin," Sloan called again, trying to find him. "Please—don't be frightened. I don't want to hurt you. I just wanted to—I just wanted to ask you some questions.

"I just wanted to tell you," Martin continued gently, now more to himself, "I just wanted to tell you what is going to happen."

He turned to see the pretty woman beside him again. He closed his eyes and ran a hand over his face, confused, bewildered.

"I don't know," he said vaguely. "I really don't know." He opened his eyes and dropped his hand. "If it's a dream—I suppose I'll wake up."

He was conscious of the laughter once more, the calliope music, the voices of the children. "I don't want it to be a dream," he said. "Oh, God, I don't want it to be a dream."

When he looked at the young woman there were tears in his eyes. "I don't want time to pass, do you understand? I want it to be the way it is now."

The young woman didn't understand what there was about this man that made her feel such pity. She wanted to comfort him, but did not know how. She watched him turn and walk out of the park, and she wondered about him all the rest of the day, this strange man with the intense look, who stood in the middle of the park, in love with it.

Martin knew where to go now. It was all he knew. Except that something odd was happening to him. Something unreal. He was not frightened. Merely disquieted. He went back to Oak Street and stood in front of his house. Again he felt memories sweep over him. He went up the front walk, up the steps and rang the bell. He was trembling and did not know why. He heard footsteps approaching, the door opened and a man looked at him through the screen.

"Yes?" the man inquired.

Martin Sloan didn't answer. For a moment he couldn't speak. Eighteen years ago he'd attended his father's funeral on a rainy, cold, wind-swept March afternoon and now he was looking into his father's face on the other side of a screen door. The square jaw, the deep-set blue eyes, the wonderfully etched lines that gave him a look of both humor and wisdom. His father's face. A face he loved. And it was looking at him through the screen.

"Yes?" His father stopped smiling and the voice became edged with impatience. "Whom did you want to see?"

Martin's voice was a whisper. "Dad! Dad!"

From inside the house he heard his mother's voice. His mother was dead fourteen years, but there was her voice. "Who is it, Robert?" his mother asked.

"Mom?" Martin's voice shook. "Is that Mom?"

Robert Sloan's eyes narrowed and his lips compressed.

"Who are you?" he asked. "What do you want here!"

Mrs. Sloan arrived at her husband's elbow, took one look at her husband's face and then stared out at Martin.

"Why are you both here?" Martin asked. "*How* can you be here?"

Questioning and concerned, Mrs. Sloan looked from Martin to her husband. "Who is it?" she asked. "What do you want, young man?"

Martin shook his head in disbelief, feeling every part of him yearn toward the man and woman who stood before him. He wanted to touch them, feel them, embrace them.

"Mom," he said finally. "Don't you know me? It's Martin, Mom. It's Martin!"

The woman's eyes grew wide. "Martin?" She turned to her husband, whispering, "He's a lunatic or something."

Robert Sloan started to close the door. Martin tried the handle. It was locked.

"Please, Dad, wait a minute. You mustn't be frightened of me. My God, how can you be frightened of me?" He pointed to himself as if he represented all the logic in the world. "I'm Martin," he repeated. "Don't you understand? I'm Martin. I grew up here."

He saw the coldness on both faces, the fear, the rejection. He was like a little boy now. He was like a little boy who had been lost and then come home and been stopped at the front door.

"I'm your son," he said. "Don't you recognize me? Mom? Dad? Please—look at me."

The door slammed shut in his face and it was several minutes before he could walk down the steps. Then he paused to look back at the house. Questions assaulted him, questions without form. Questions that made no sense. What in God's name was happening here? Where was he? When was he? Trees and houses converged on him and he felt the street coming up at him. Oh God, he didn't want to leave. He had to see his parents again. He had to talk to them.

The sound of a car horn intruded upon him. In the next yard, there was a kid who seemed familiar. He was standing beside a roadster with a rumble seat.

"Hi," the boy shouted at him.

"Hi," Martin answered. He went toward the car.

"Nice, huh?" the boy asked. "First one of its kind in town. My dad just bought it for me."

"What?" Martin asked.

"New car," the boy's smile was persistent. "First one of its kind. Beauty, huh?"

Martin looked from the front bumper to the rear light. "Got a rumble seat," he said softly.

The boy tilted his head questioningly. "Sure, it's got a rumble seat. It's a roadster."

"I haven't seen a rumble seat in twenty years."

There was a silence and the boy's face tried to recapture the enthusiasm of a moment before. "Where you been, mister? Siberia?"

Martin Sloan didn't answer him. He just stared at the roadster. First one of its kind in town, the boy had said. First one. Brand new. A 1934 automobile and it was brand new.

It was night when Martin Sloan returned to Oak Street and stood in front of his house looking at the incredibly warm lights that shone from within. The crickets were a million tambourines that came out of the darkness. There was a scent of hyacinth in the air. There was a quiet rustle of leaf-laden trees that screened out the moon and made odd shadows on cooling sidewalks. There was a feeling of summer, so well remembered.

Martin Sloan had walked a lot of pavements and thought a lot of thoughts. He knew now with a clear and precise clarity that he was back twenty years in time. He had somehow, inexplicably, breached an unbreachable dimension. He was no longer disturbed nor apprehensive. He had a purpose now and a resolve. He wanted to put in a claim to the past. He went toward the front steps and his foot hit something soft. It was a baseball glove. He picked it up, slipped it on his hand, pounded the pocket as he had years ago. Then he discovered a bicycle propped up in the middle of the yard. He rang the bell on the handlebar and felt a hand enclose his and muffle the ring. He looked up to see Robert Sloan beside him.

"Back again, huh?" his father said.

"I had to come back, Pop. This is my house." He held up the glove in his hand. "This is mine, too. You bought it for me on my eleventh birthday."

His father's eyes narrowed.

"You gave me a baseball, too," Martin continued. "It had Lou Gehrig's autograph on it."

His father stared at him for a long, reflective moment. "Who are you?" he asked softly. "What do you want here?" He struck a match, lit his pipe, then held the match out while he studied Martin's face in the brief flame.

"I just want to rest," Martin said. "I just want to stop running for a while. I belong here. Don't you understand, Pop? I belong here."

Robert Sloan's face softened. He was a kind man and a sensitive one. And wasn't there something about this stranger which gave him an odd feeling? Something about him that—that looked familiar?

"Look, son," he said. "You're probably sick. You've got delusions or something, maybe. I don't want to hurt you and I don't want you to get in any trouble either. But you'd better get out of here or there *will* be trouble."

There was the sound of the screen door behind him opening and Mrs. Sloan came out.

"Who are you talking to, Rob—" she began to call. She stopped abruptly when she saw Martin.

He ran over to the porch and up the steps to grab her. "Mom," he shouted at her. "Look at me! Look into my face. You can tell, can't you?"

Mrs. Sloan looked frightened and tried to back away.

"Mom! *Look at me.* Please! Who am I? Tell me who I am."

"You're a stranger," Mrs. Sloan said. "I've never seen you before. Robert, tell him to go away."

Martin grabbed her again and turned her around to face him. "You've got a son named Martin, haven't you?

He goes to Emerson Public School. The month of August he spends at his aunt's farm near Buffalo, and a couple of summers you've gone up to Saratoga Lake and rented a cottage there. And once I had a sister and she died when she was a year old."

Mrs. Sloan stared at him wide-eyed. "Where's Martin now?" she said to her husband.

Again Martin tightened his grip on her shoulders. *"I'm Martin,"* he shouted. "I'm your son! You've got to believe me. I'm your son Martin." He released her and reached into his coat pocket to pull out his wallet. He began to tear out cards. "See? See? All my cards are in here. All my identification. Read them. Go ahead, read them."

He tried to force the wallet on her and his mother, desperate and frightened, lashed out and slapped him across the face. It was an instinctive action, done with all her strength. Martin stood stock still, the wallet slipping out of his fingers to fall to the ground, his head shaking from side to side as if a terrible mistake had been made and he was amazed that the woman couldn't perceive it. From the distance came the sound of the calliope. Martin turned to listen. He walked down the steps past his father to the front walk. He stood there for a moment listening to the calliope again. Then he began to run down the middle of the street toward the sound of the music.

"Martin," he shouted, as he raced toward the park. "Martin! Martin! Martin, I've got to talk to you!"

The park was lit up with lanterns and street lights and colored electric signs on the stands. A moving path of light from the merry-go-round went round and round and played on Martin's face as he looked wildly around to find an eleven-year-old boy in a night filled with them. Then suddenly he saw him. He was riding the merry-go-round.

Martin raced over to it, grabbed a post as it whirled past and catapulted himself on to the moving platform. He started a running, stumbling journey through a maze of bobbing horses and a hundred little faces that moved up and down.

"Martin," he shouted, colliding with a horse. "Martin, please, I have to talk to you!"

The little boy heard his name, looked over his shoulder, saw the man with the disheveled hair and perspiring face coming toward him. He climbed off the horse, threw his box of popcorn away and started to run, threading his way expertly among the rising and dipping horses.

"Martin!" Sloan's voice called after him.

He was getting closer. He was only ten or fifteen feet away now, but the boy continued to run from him.

It happened suddenly. Martin came within an arms' length of the boy and reached out to grab him. The boy looked over his shoulder and, unseeing, stepped over the edge of the platform and fell headlong into whirling, multicolored space. His leg caught on a protruding piece of metal that extended from under the platform, and for a shrieking, agonizing moment he was dragged along with the merry-go-round. The boy screamed just once before the attendant, his face a pale mask, reached for the clutch and pulled it back. No one noticed then or remembered later that two screams joined the calliope music as it died away in a dissonant, premature finale. Two screams. One from an eleven-year-old boy, descending through a nightmare, before he blacked out. One from Martin Sloan who felt a piercing agony shoot through his right leg. He clutched at it, almost falling. There were shouts now from mothers and children as they raced toward the little boy lying a few feet from the merry-go-round, face down in the dirt. They collected around him. An attendant pushed his way through and kneeled by the boy. He gently lifted him in his arms and a little girl's high-pitched voice rose over the crowd.

"Look at his leg. Look at his leg."

Martin Sloan, aged eleven was carried out of the park, his right leg bleeding and mutilated. Martin tried to reach him but already they had carried him off. There was a silence and then a murmur of voices. People began to drift out of the area to their homes. Concession stands closed up. Lights went off. Within a moment Martin found himself alone. He leaned his head against one of the guard poles of the merry-go-round and closed his eyes.

"I only wanted to tell you," he whispered. "I only wanted to tell you that this was the wonderful time for you. Don't let any of it go by without—without enjoying it. There won't be any more merry-go-rounds. No more cotton candy. No more band concerts. I only wanted to tell you, Martin, that this is the wonderful time. Now! Here! That's all. That's all I wanted to tell you."

He felt a sadness well up inside of him. "God help me, Martin, that's all I wanted to tell you!"

He went over to the edge of the platform and sat down. Wooden horses stared lifelessly at him. Shuttered concession stands surveyed him blindly. The summer night hung all around him and let him alone. He didn't know how long he had sat there when he heard footsteps. He looked up to see his father walk across the merry-go-round platform to reach his side. Robert Sloan looked down at him and held out a wallet in his hand. Martin's wallet.

"I thought you'd want to know," Robert said. "The boy will be all right. He may limp some, the doctor told us, but he'll be all right."

Martin nodded. "I thank God for that."

"You dropped this by the house," Robert said, handing him the wallet. "I looked inside."

"And?"

"It told quite a few things about you," Robert said earnestly. "The driver's license, cards, the money in it." He paused for a moment. "It seems that you *are* Martin Sloan. You're thirty-six years old. You have an apartment in New York." Then, with a question in his voice— "It says your license expires in 1960. That's twenty-five years from now. The dates on the bills—the money, those dates haven't arrived yet, either."

Martin looked straight in his father's face. "You know now then, don't you?" he asked.

Robert nodded. "Yes, I know. I know who you are and I know you've come a long way from here. A long way and—a long time. I don't know why or how. Do you?"

Martin shook his head.

"But you know other things, don't you, Martin? Things that will happen."

"Yes, I do."

"You also know when your mother and I—when we'll—"

Martin whispered, "Yes, I know that, too."

Robert took the pipe out of his mouth and studied Martin for a long moment. "Well, don't tell me. I'd appreciate not knowing. That's a part of the mystery we live with. I think it should always be a mystery." There was a moment's pause. "Martin?"

"Yes, Dad."

Robert put his hand on Martin's shoulder. "You have to leave here. There's no room for you. And there's no place. Do you understand?"

Martin nodded and said softly, "I see that now. But I *don't* understand. Why not?"

Robert smiled. "I guess because we only get one chance. Maybe there's only one summer to a customer." Now his voice was deep and rich with compassion. "The little boy . . . the one *I* know, the one who belongs here. This is his summer, Martin. Just as it was yours one time." He shook his head. "Don't make him share it."

Martin rose and looked off toward the darkened park.

"Is it so bad—where you're from?" Robert asked him.

"I thought so," Martin answered. "I've been living at a dead run, Dad. I've been weak and I made believe I was strong. I've been scared to death—but I've been playing a strong man. And suddenly it all caught up with me. And I felt so tired, Pop. I felt so damned tired, running for so long. Then—one day I knew I had to come back. I had to come back and get on a merry-go-round and listen to a band concert and eat cotton candy. I had to stop and breathe and close my eyes and smell and listen."

"I guess we all want that," Robert said gently. "But, Martin, when you go back, maybe you'll find that there are merry-go-rounds and band concerts where you are and summer nights, too. Maybe you haven't looked in the right place. You've been looking behind you, Martin. Try looking ahead."

There was a silence. Martin turned to look at his father. He felt a love, an acme of tenderness, a link, deeper than flesh that ties men to men.

"Maybe, Dad," he said. "Maybe. Good-by, Dad."

Robert walked several feet away, stopped, remained there for a moment, his back to Martin, then he turned toward him again. "Good-by—son," he said.

An instant later he was gone. Behind Martin the merry-go-round began to move. The lights were off, there was no noise, only the shadowy figures of the horses going round and round. Martin stepped on it as it turned, a quiet herd of wooden steeds with painted eyes that went around in the night. It went a full circle and then began to slow down. There was no one on it. Martin Sloan was gone.

Martin Sloan went into the drugstore. It was the one he remembered as a boy, but aside from the general shape of the room and the stairway leading to an office off a small balcony, it bore no resemblance to the place he remembered. It was light and cheerful with strips of fluorescent lights, a blaring, garish juke box, a fancy soda bar full of shining chrome. There were a lot of high school kids there dancing to the juke box, poring over the teen mags in the corner near the front window. It was air conditioned and very cool. Martin walked through the smoke of cigarettes, the blaring rock-'n-roll, the laughing voices of the kids, his eyes looking around trying to find any single thing that had familiarity. A young soda jerk behind the counter smiled at him.

"Hi," he said. "Something for you?"

Martin sat down on one of the chrome and leather stools.

"Maybe a chocolate soda, huh?" he said to the kid behind the fountain. "Three dips?"

"Three dips?" the soda jerk repeated. "Sure, I can make one with three dips for you. It'll be extra. Thirty-five cents. Okay?"

Martin smiled a little sadly. "Thirty-five cents, huh?" His eyes scanned the room again. "How about old Mr. Wilson," he asked. "Used to own this place."

"Oh, he died," the soda jerk said. "A long time ago. Maybe fifteen, twenty years. What kind of ice cream you want? Chocolate? Vanilla?"

Martin wasn't listening to him.

"Vanilla?" the soda jerk repeated.

"I've changed my mind," Martin said. "I guess I'll pass on the soda." He started to get off the stool and half stumbled as his stiff right leg was thrust out momentarily in an awkward position. "These stools weren't built for bum legs," he said with a rueful grin.

The soda jerk looked concerned. "Guess not. Get that in the war?"

"What?"

"Your leg. Did you get that in the war?"

"No," said Martin thoughtfully. "As a matter of fact I got it falling off a merry-go-round when I was a kid. Freak thing."

The soda jerk snapped his fingers. "The merry-go-round! Hey, I remember the merry-go-round. They tore it down a few years ago. Condemned it." Then he smiled sympathetically. "Little late I guess, huh?"

"How's that?" Martin asked.

"A little late for you, I mean."

Martin took a long look around the drugstore. "Very late," he said softly. "Very late for me."

He went out into the hot summer day again. The hot summer day that appeared on the calendar as June 26, 1959. He walked down the main street and out of the town, back toward the gas station, where he'd left his car for a lube job and oil change so long ago. He walked slowly, his right leg dragging slightly along the dusty shoulder of the highway.

At the gas station he paid the attendant, got into his car, turned it around and started back toward New York City. Only once did he glance over his shoulder at a sign which read, "Homewood, 1 1/2 miles." The sign was wrong. He knew that much. Homewood was farther away than that. It was much farther.

The tall man in the Brooks Brothers suit, driving a red Mercedes-Benz, gripped the wheel thoughtfully as he headed south toward New York. He didn't know exactly what would face him at the other end of the journey. All he knew was that he'd discovered something. Homewood. Homewood, New York. It wasn't walking distance.

From Rod Serling's closing narration, "Walking Distance," The Twilight Zone, October 30, 1959, CBS Television Network.

LONG ANGLE SHOT

Looking down as the car slowly starts onto the highway. Over the disappearing car we hear the Narrator's Voice.

NARRATOR'S VOICE

Martin Sloan, age thirty-six. Vice
president in charge of media.
Successful in most things, but
not in the one effort that all
men try at some time in their lives—
trying to go home again.
      (a pause)
And also like all men perhaps
there'll be an occasion, maybe
a summer night sometime, when he'll
look up from what he's doing and
listen to the distant music of
a calliope—and hear the voices
and the laughter of the people and
the places of his past. And perhaps
across his mind there'll flit a
little errant wish—that a man
might not have to become old,
never outgrow the parks and the
merry-go-rounds of his youth.
      (a pause)

And he'll smile then too because
he'll know it *is* just an errant
wish. Some wisp of memory not
too important really. Some laughing ghosts that cross a man's
mind . . . that are a part of The
Twilight Zone.

Now the CAMERA PANS down the road to the sign
that reads "Homewood, 1 1/2 miles."

FADE TO BLACK

The Fever

It was this way with Franklin Gibbs. He had a carefully planned, precisely wrought little life that encompassed a weekly Kiwanis meeting on Thursday evening at the Salinas Hotel; an adult study group sponsored by his church on Wednesday evening; church each Sunday morning; his job as a teller at the local bank; and about one evening a week spent with friends playing parchesi or something exciting like that. He was a thin, erect, middle-aged, little man whose narrow shoulders were constantly kept pinned back in the manner of a West Point plebe and he wore a tight fitting vest which spanned a pigeon chest. On his lapel was a Kiwanis ten-year attendance pin and, above that, a fifteen-year service pin given him by the president of the bank. He and his wife lived in a small, two-bedroom house on Elm Street, which was about twenty years old, had a small garden in back, and an arbor of roses in front which were Mr. Gibbs's passion.

Flora Gibbs, married to Franklin for twenty-two years, was angular, with mousy, stringy hair and chest measurements perhaps a quarter of an inch smaller than her husband's. She was quiet voiced though talkative, long, if unconsciously, suffering and had led a life devoted to the care and feeding of Franklin Gibbs, the placating of his sullen moods, his finicky appetite, and his uncontrollable rage at any change in the routine of their daily lives.

This background explains at least in part Franklin Gibbs's violent reaction to Flora's winning the contest. It was one of those crazy and unexpected things that seem occasionally to explode into an otherwise prosaic, uneventful life. And it had exploded into Flora's. She had written in to a national contest explaining in exactly eighteen words why she preferred Aunt Martha's ready-mix biscuits to any other brand. She had written concisely and sparingly, because her life was a concise and spare life without the frills or the little, flamboyant luxuries of other women, a life of rationed hours and budgeted moments; thin, skimpy, unadorned, unpunctuated, until the contest, by the remotest hint of variance or color. And then she got the telegram. Not the first prize—that would have been too much. (It happened to be fifty thousand dollars, and Franklin, with thin-lipped impatience, suggested that perhaps had she tried harder she might have won it.) It was the third prize, which involved a three-day trip for two, all expenses paid, to Las Vegas, Nevada, a beautiful room in a most exceptionally modern and famous gambling hotel, with shows, sightseeing tours, and wonderful food all thrown in, along with an airplane flight there and back.

The announcement of the trip fell into Flora's life like a star shell bursting over a no-man's land. Even Franklin was momentarily taken aback at the suddenly animated appearance of his normally drab-faced wife. It gradually dawned on him that Flora was quite serious about wanting to take the trip to Vegas. There was a scene over the breakfast table the morning after the telegram's arrival. Franklin told his wife in no uncertain terms that gambling in Las Vegas was for the very rich or the very foolish. It was not for the stable or the moral and since morality and stability meant a great deal to Mr. Gibbs, they would have to telegraph back to the contest people (collect, Mr. Gibbs parenthetically noted) to acquaint them with their decision about Las Vegas, Nevada and, as Mr. Gibbs put it, "its decidedly questionable roadhouse vicedens."

When Mr. Gibbs returned from the bank that noontime for lunch, there wasn't any. Flora was crying in her room and, for the first time in a rooster-pecked, subservient, acquiescent life, she took a stand. She had won the trip to Las Vegas and she was going, with or without Franklin. This information was imparted through heavy sobbing and a spasmodic rendition of a biblical quotation—something about whither thou goest I shalt go; something some lady in the Old Testament had said to another lady, but sufficiently close in its application here to cover a husband not accompanying his wife on a trip to Las Vegas. But actually it was a combination of a long Memorial Day weekend and the fact that the trip was free that finally made Franklin Gibbs change his mind.

A week later, Franklin, in his shiny, tight, blue Kiwanis Officer's Installation suit with vest and lapel button, and Flora, in a flower-patterned cotton dress with a big green sash and a flower-pot hat with a large feather, took the six-and-a-half-hour flight to Las Vegas, Nevada. Flora spent the entire six-and-a-half hours gurgling excitedly; Franklin remained petulantly silent with only an occasional remark about any state government so totally immoral as to permit legalized gambling.

They were met at the airport by a hotel car which drove them to the Desert Frontier Palace—a gaudy, low-slung, sweeping structure emblazoned with nude girls in neon. Flora spent the automobile trip telling the driver all about Elgin, Kansas, in a high-pitched, ludicrously girlish way. Franklin remained silent except for a single comment on a platinum blonde who passed in front of the car when it stopped for a light. This was to the effect that she seemed typical of a town of decidedly questionable virtue.

Their room was air-conditioned, very modern and comfortable in a highly chromed way. The management had left a bowl of fruit and a vase of flowers which Flora nervously rearranged three or four times, while she chattered at her husband. Franklin sat glumly reading a Chamber of Commerce booklet from the City Fathers of Las Vegas, punctuating the few silences with negative comparisons between Vegas and the much more solid, if smaller, Elgin, Kansas.

An hour later there was a knock on the door and the hotel public relations man entered with a photographer. His name was Marty Lubow and he wore the professional greeter's smile with competence.

"Well, Mr. and Mrs. Gibbs," Lubow asked, "is your room comfortable? Is there anything at all you need? Anything I can do for you?"

Flora's voice trilled nervously as her hands darted around her dress, pulling up, yanking down, straightening, smoothing. "Oh, it's lovely, Mr. Lubow. Just lovely. You make us feel—well, you make us feel important!"

Lubow laughed jovially back at her, "Well, after all, you are important, Mrs. Gibbs. It isn't every day we can entertain a celebrated contest winner!"

The photographer at his elbow looked glum and whispered over his shoulder, "Not every day—maybe every *other* day."

Lubow's laugh covered the photographer's voice and pushed its way through the room. There was something enveloping about Mr. Lubow's laugh. It was his own special weapon for every emergency.

"I think," he said, "we should take our pictures right here. I think standing in the middle of the room would be best, don't you, Joe?"

The photographer heaved a deep sigh which was a combination of agreement and resignation. He stuck a bulb in the flash section of the camera, then leaned against the door lining up the shot. Lubow ushered Flora to a spot in the center of the room, then beckoned to Franklin who remained silently dour in his chair.

"Right over here next to your lovely missus, Mr. Gibbs," he said happily.

Franklin let out a long-suffering sigh, rose and walked over to stand close to Flora.

"Wonderful," gushed Lubow, looking at the two of them with amazed eyes, as if by joining them in the center of the room he had performed a feat only a degree less amazing than climbing the Matterhorn all alone. "Just wonderful," he repeated. "All right, Joe, how's that look?"

The photographer responded by taking the picture and left both Flora and Franklin blinking in the aftermath of the flash—Flora with her fixed, nervous smile, and Franklin staring malevolently and challengingly toward the photographer. Again Lubow's laughter shook the room. He pounded on Franklin's back, wrung his hand, patted Flora's cheek and somehow, in the same motion, headed toward the door. The photographer had already opened it and was on his way out.

"Now you folks just keep in touch with us—" Lubow was saying as he left.

"It's *The Elgin Bugle,* Mr. Lubow," Flora called after him.

Lubow turned. "How's that?" he inquired.

"That's our home town paper," Flora answered. *"The Elgin Bugle."*

"Of course, of course, Mrs. Gibbs. *The Elgin Bugle.* We'll send a copy of the picture right out to them. Enjoy yourselves, folks, and welcome to Las Vegas and the Desert Frontier Palace."

He winked happily at Flora, grinned manfully at Franklin and was only momentarily nonplussed by the frozen petulance on Franklin's face. He recovered sufficiently to wave as he walked away. His laughter was a twenty-one-gun salute honoring nothing in particular, but in an odd way pulling the curtain down on the meeting.

It was another fifty-five minutes before Flora could persuade her husband to go out to the gambling room and see what it was like. It took the bulk of those minutes for her to persuade him that there was nothing immoral in just *watching* people gambling. And in the intervals between argument she was forced to listen to Franklin's own personal critique on the miserable weakness of human beings who threw away money on dice, cards and machines. In the end he suffered himself to be put into his Kiwanis Officer Installation coat once again and led by Flora into the main building of the hotel, and then into the principal gambling room. It was a plush, noisy, people-loaded room, crowded with crap tables, a long bar, roulette wheels and three rows of one-armed bandits. It was a room full of noises that rose up from the heavily carpeted floor, touched the accoustical ceiling, and though softened by both, nonetheless hung in the air. The noises were gambling noises. There was the spinning clatter of roulette wheels. The tinkle of glasses. The metallic clack, clack, clack of the one-armed bandit levers being pulled down. There were the droning voices of the croupiers calling out numbers, red and black, and underneath all of this the varied pitch of human voices—the nervous squeals of the winners, the protesting groans of the losers. The sounds fused together and hit Franklin and Flora Gibbs with the force of an explosion as they entered the room and stood there on the periphery of the activity, staring into the strange, gaudy and noisy new world.

The two of them stood at the door trying to feel at ease, conscious for the first time of how they looked—Flora, a fluttery woman, in an unfashionable dress with a corsage that did nothing but emphasize dullness; Franklin, a little man in a 1937 suit, with slicked-down hair, pointed shoes and a look of mid-western primness, worn defensively like a badge. They were two foreign elements at this moment, joined together in a bond of inferiority closer, perhaps, than they ever shared in Elgin, Kansas.

They stood there like that for ten minutes, watching the tables, the games, the stacks of chips and silver dollars; the glamorous-looking women and the impeccable men. Flora's eyes grew wider and wider. She turned to Franklin.

"It has such a flavor, this place!"

He looked at her, fishy-eyed, then turned up his nose. "Flavor, Flora? I'm surprised at you. You know how I feel about gambling."

Flora smiled appeasingly. "Well, this is different though, Franklin—"

"It is neither different nor moral. Gambling is gambling! It's *your* vacation, Flora. But I must, in good conscience, repeat to you what I have been saying all along— that it's a tragic waste of time. Hear me, Flora? A tragic waste of time!"

Flora's lower lip trembled and she reached out to touch his arm. "Please, Franklin," she said quietly, "try to enjoy it, won't you? We haven't had a vacation in such a long time. Such a very long time. A vacation—or even a good time together."

Franklin's left eyebrow shot upward and his voice was that of a wounded Congressional Medal of Honor winner who had suddenly been told he had to go back on the line. "It is a matter of record, Flora," he announced, "that I work desperately hard and I have very little time—" It was the opening paragraph to a tailor-made speech that Franklin delivered at least once a month. It was when he branched off into a new tack, alleging that he felt unclean in this kind of room with semi-clad girls and dice throwers, that he realized Flora was no longer listening to him.

Across the room a one-armed bandit had lit up, a bell clanged, and a woman screamed hysterically. After a moment, a long-legged blonde in tights, carrying a basket of money, walked over to the woman by the machine, called out its number to a floor manager and then handed the woman the basket of money. She was immediately surrounded by members of her party who took her to the bar, all chattering like happy squirrels.

Flora left Franklin's side and went to the one-armed bandits spread along one whole side of the room. From where she stood it looked like a forest of arms yanking down levers. There was a continuous clack, clack, clack of levers, then a click, click, click of tumblers coming up. Following this was a metallic poof sometimes followed by the clatter of silver dollars coming down through the funnel to land with a happy smash in the coin receptacle at the bottom of the machine.

Franklin was studying the long-legged blonde with sour disapproval, and was unaware that Flora had taken a nickel out of her purse until she dropped the coin into one of the machines. Flora was reaching for the lever when she realized that Franklin was glaring at her. She flushed, forced a smile and then looked supplicating at him.

"Franklin, it's—it's only a nickel machine, dear."

His high-pitched voice sandpapered against her. "Just a nickel machine, Flora? *Just* a nickel machine! Why don't you just go out and throw handfuls of nickels into the street?"

"Franklin, darling—"

He moved closer to her, his voice low, but full of a carefully closeted fury. "All right, Flora, we go to Las Vegas. We waste three days and two nights. We do it because that's your idiotic way of enjoying yourself. And it doesn't cost us anything. But now you're spending our money. Not even spending it, Flora—you're just throwing it away. And it's at this point, Flora, that I have to take a hand. You are obviously not mature enough—"

There was the suggestion of pain in Flora's eyes. Her face was edged with a nervousness that Franklin recognized as a prelude to several hours of quiet hand-wringing, and deep, spasmodic sighs. It was Flora's only defense over the years.

"Please . . . please, Franklin, don't make a scene," she whispered. "I won't play. I promise you—" She turned to the machine and then, with a kind of hopeless gesture, back to him. "The nickel's already in."

Franklin heaved a deep, resigned sigh and looked up toward the ceiling. "All right," he said. "Throw it away. Pull down the lever or whatever it is you do. Just throw it away."

Flora kept her eyes on Franklin as she pulled the lever down, listening to the sound of the tumblers and then the empty poof and then the silence. The corners of Franklin's mouth twitched in a righteous smile, and for one fleeting moment Flora hated him. Then habit took over for her, and she stood quietly at her husband's elbow and heard him declare that he was going back to the room to get ready for dinner.

"I guess I'm not very lucky," she said softly.

He didn't answer. At the door she looked straight into his face.

"Franklin, it was only a nickel."

"Twenty of them make a dollar, Flora, and I work hard for those dollars!"

He was about to open the door when a drunk standing by a dollar machine turned and saw him. The drunk grabbed Franklin, pulled him over to the machine. Franklin recoiled as if exposed to something infective, but the drunk held Franklin firmly with one hand, a glass in the other.

"Here, old buddy," the drunk said, "—you try it." He put down his glass and took a silver dollar from his pocket. "Here, go ahead. I'm one hour and thirty minutes on this miserable, crummy, money-grabbin'—!" He forced the silver dollar into Franklin's hand. "Go ahead, old pal. It's yours. You play it."

A woman at the bar waved frantically at them. "Charlie," she screamed, "are you gonna come over here or am I gonna come over there and get you?"

"I'm coming, honey, I'm coming," he answered. He smiled at Franklin, burped out a shaft of Johnny Walker-flavored air, patted Franklin on the back and then guided his hand, still holding the silver dollar, into the slot on top of the machine.

Franklin looked like a small animal caught in a trap. He looked wildly left and right, searching for aid, embarrassed, discomfited, frightened.

"Really," Franklin said, "I'm not at all interested. Please—I'm in a hurry—"

The drunk chortled happily as the silver dollar was deposited in the slot, then walked unsteadily toward the bar.

Franklin glowered at the machine. His first thought was the possibility of getting the silver dollar back without having to play it. He studied the machine intently. It was like all the others. Big, gaudily lit, with a glass-covered compartment in the center, showing an incredible number of silver dollars inside its big metal gut. Two lights over this compartment had an odd similarity to eyes and the slot at the bottom filled out the picture of a monstrous neon face. Franklin raised his right hand to the lever. Over his shoulder he saw Flora smiling hopefully. Then, as if taking a big decisive step, he yanked down the lever, watched the whirling tumblers that one after another came to a stop, showing two cherries and a lemon. There was a loud metallic clack and then the sound of the coins as they arrived in the receptacle at the bottom —ten of them.

Franklin was only faintly aware of Flora's delighted squeal. He looked down at the coins and slowly, one by one, took them out. A strange, warm sensation was running through him; an odd excitement that he'd never experienced before. He saw his reflection in the chrome strip on the machine and was surprised at what he saw—a flushed, bright-eyed little face, cheek muscles twitching, lips stretched tight in a thin smile.

"Oh, Franklin, you *are* lucky."

He looked at Flora, manufacturing a grimness of face and tone and held up the silver dollars in his palm. He said, "Now, Flora, you'll see the difference between a normal, mature, thoughtful man and these wild idiots around here. We will take these, put them in our room, and we will go home with them."

"Of course, dear."

"These baboons here would throw it away. They'd compulsively put it back into the machine. But the Gibbses don't! The Gibbses know the value of money! Come on, my dear, it's late. I'd like to shave for dinner."

Without waiting for her, he turned toward the door. Flora padded after him like a diffident pet. A look of pride was on her face as she watched the tiny, erect figure ahead of her pushing his way through the crowd with a resolution and a strength that seemed to reaffirm the status of Elgin, Kansas. Neither of them saw the drunk return to the machine and put in another silver dollar. But Franklin heard the sound of coins landing in the receptacle.

He whirled around, startled. He had heard coins all right, but he had heard something else too. He had distinctly heard his own name, a metallic, raspy jumbled rendition—but, nonetheless, his name. The coins had landed in the receptacle and had called out, "Franklin." He rubbed nervously at his jaw and turned to Flora.

"Did you say something?" he asked.

"What, dear?"

"Did you call my name, Flora?"

"Why no, dear."

Franklin looked over toward the machine again, puzzled. The drunk was weaving his way back toward the bar and the machine was unattended.

"I could have sworn—" Franklin began. Then he shook

his head. But he studied the machine for one more moment. It *did* resemble a face, the two lights were eyes, the glass-covered square in the center with the silver dollars inside—that was the nose. And the opening at the bottom where the money came down—that was the odd little mouth with the protuberant lower lip.

"Like a face," he said aloud.

"What is, dear?" Flora asked.

"That silly-looking machine. It's like a face."

Flora turned to stare at it blankly then she looked back at Franklin. "A face?" she inquired.

"Never mind," said Franklin. "Let's get ready for dinner."

All the way back to the room Franklin pondered over the experience of hearing a machine call out his name. It was ridiculous, of course, he realized. It hadn't really happened. It had been a combination of voices and sounds and his own imagination, but it had been real enough to startle him, to jar him at that moment. But he was not the least bit frightened by what had happened. Indeed, he felt a sensation of strength and accomplishment. He'd beaten that ugly machine.

He, Franklin Gibbs, had walked into the arena of the enemy, spit in the eye of immorality, turned his back and walked away. It was a triumph of Good. What he didn't admit to himself as he shaved his severe little face, was that the victory had been too ephemeral. Too quick. Too fleeting. Franklin Gibbs, though he would never admit it aloud at this moment, wanted to go back into the arena!

They had dinner and saw part of the early show. Franklin was upset because the waiter had put chives in his baked potato without asking him and he'd always hated chives. They never got to see Frank Sinatra because the opening comedian was too dirty. Flora giggled nervously at some of the things he said, not fully understanding them, then glancing at Franklin apologetically. Franklin sat stiffly upright, unsmiling and disapproving. When the eight girls in black sequins were half-way through the second dance number, he arose, nodded tersely at Flora, and started out. Unquestioning, Flora followed him.

At ten o'clock they were in bed. Franklin had delivered a most comprehensive critique on foul-mouthed comedians and dirty little sluts off the street who became dancers. He had brushed his teeth, performed the ritual of an alcohol rub in his hair, using a special medicine prepared for him by their Elgin druggist, brushed off perfunctorily Flora's suggestion that they might visit the gambling room once again, just to observe, and gone to bed. Flora fell asleep almost immediately as she always did. Franklin, on the other hand, lay with hands behind his head, staring up at the ceiling. There was a small night light by the door and it sent a very low orange gleam into the darkness of the room. The silver dollars were stacked up on top of the dresser in front of the mirror. At intervals Franklin's eyes would move down so that he could look across the foot of the bed to the stack of coins. He was getting drowsy and was almost asleep when he heard the sound again.

"Franklin!"

It was coins tumbling together out of a machine and calling out his name, "Franklin!" It happened three times in a row before he sat upright in bed looking around. It was an odd indefinable kind of sound. The closest thing to it Franklin could imagine was if his name had been pronounced by a robot. He looked at the coins on the dresser and was mildly surprised that the pile seemed to look higher, more than ten coins now. It was as if there were twenty silver dollars piled on top of one another. And the longer he looked at them the higher the pile seemed to grow.

He got out of bed and walked over to the dresser. He picked up the coins and juggled them in his hand. There was a nice feeling to silver dollars in the hand, he decided. A nice heavy feeling. He caught sight of himself in the mirror, and felt vaguely disturbed by what he saw. The Franklin Gibbs that stared back at him wore a face of greed and avarice; of a compulsive hunger, a lecherous, naked desire. It was not his face at all except in broad outline.

Flora was suddenly awake. "Is anything the matter, dear?" she asked.

"There is nothing the matter," he said, forcing an

evenness to his tone, "except—" He held out the silver dollars in his hand. "This is tainted money, Flora. It is absolutely immoral. Nothing good can come of money won like this. I'm going back inside and feed it back into the machine. Get rid of it."

Flora slowly lay back in bed, dulled by sleep. "All right, dear," she murmured, "You do what you think best."

She was asleep by the time Franklin had put his clothes back on and was combing his hair in front of the dresser mirror.

"If there's one thing that I understand extremely well, Flora," he said to his sleeping wife across the room, "it's morality! And I will not have tainted money smelling up our pockets. I am definitely going back in there and get rid of it." He turned to her, "Now go back to sleep, Flora."

She was breathing regularly in measured rhythm. Franklin turned back to the mirror and straightened his coat, picked up the silver dollars, smiled at them, and then, feeling the excitement rise in him again, walked out toward the big room that never went to sleep.

Three hours later Franklin stood by the machine, his tie knot pulled down, his shirt unbuttoned, his coat open. He was unconscious of time or noise or the way he looked or anything else. His whole existence had resolved itself into a simple set of actions. Put the coin in. Pull down the lever. Watch and wait. Put the coin in. Pull down the lever. Watch and wait. Study the tumblers and hold your breath. A cherry always meant something in the way of a return. Lemons were death. The strip of writing like a label appeared only in a few winning combinations. The bells were hopeful, but you needed three of them to make it worth your while and the plums weren't any good at all. He didn't know or care that all of his carefully wrought and conceived standards, his entire frame of reference, everything he'd ever stood for or purported to stand for, had now been shoved down a drain some place. What was important to him were cherries and bells and plums and the combination of them as they appeared when the tumblers stopped.

He kept feeding the machine the coins and pulling down the lever and studying the machine and pulling down the lever and feeding and pulling and feeding and pulling. Three times he went to the cashier's desk to break bills, always nervously watching over his shoulder to make certain no one would take his machine. Each time, after he'd collected the silver dollars, he would literally run back over to the one-armed bandit and even this didn't register with him as not being the sort of thing Franklin Gibbs would have done in Elgin, Kansas, twenty-four hours earlier.

At two in the morning Franklin Gibbs still didn't know what was happening to him. The clammy sweat of fatigue ran down his face and clung to his pores. He found his body jerking spasmodically as the tumblers came up one after another. His stomach felt empty and drained. He was aware that he was losing a great deal of money. How much he wasn't sure—he didn't allow himself to figure it out. All he knew as a certainty was that he, Franklin Gibbs, would never be defeated by a filthy, immoral machine. And beyond that, he wanted silver dollars. He wanted them desperately. He wanted to listen to the click of the machine and then the exciting clatter of coins rubbing against themselves as they flooded out of the machine. He wanted to load his pockets with them and feel them, bulky and heavy against his body. He wanted to reach into his pockets and run his sweaty fingers over them.

So he continued to play and at three-thirty in the morning Franklin Gibbs was a desperate little man with a stiff, sore right arm and an obsession that blocked out the rest of the world and left him standing by a one-armed bandit feeding it coins. Winning three, losing five. Winning two, losing three. Winning six, then losing ten.

A half-hour later Flora came, her face a contradiction of sleep and concern. She had awakened to find the bed empty and hadn't remembered her conversation with Franklin prior to his leaving the room. Her eyes went wide when she saw him standing close by the machine. She had never seen her husband look this way. His suit was rumpled, his shirt sweat-stained, his face, under a growing beard stubble, was oyster white. There was a glazed quality to the eyes and it was almost as if he were looking through her rather than at her. She nervously approached him in time to hear him scream.

"Well, damn it!"

The tumblers showed a plum, a lemon and a bell. There had been the loud metallic click of defeat and the intense, somber face of her husband had a wild quality.

Flora touched his sleeve and said softly, "Franklin, dear, it's terribly late."

He turned to stare at her, taking a moment to identify her, having to reach back into his subconscious to reconstitute a world that he had left several hours before and which no longer seemed very real to him.

"Stay here, Flora," he said. "I have to get some more silver dollars. Don't let anybody use this machine, understand?"

"Franklin, dear—" her voice half-heartedly chased him, and then died out as he left her behind.

She watched him take a bill out of his wallet, hand it to the cashier, and get a large stack of silver dollars in return. He carried them back, brushed past her and started to feed them into the machine, one by one. He'd gone through five of them with no result when Flora touched his arm again, this time much more positively, and with a grip sufficiently tight to keep him from depositing yet another silver dollar.

"Franklin!" her voice carried a rising concern. "How much money have you lost? Have you been playing this machine all night?"

Franklin's voice was terse. "I have."

"You've lost a great deal of money then, haven't you?"

"Very likely."

Flora wet her lips and tried to smile. "Well, darling, don't you think you ought to stop?"

He looked at her as if she'd just suggested that he drink a bucket of paint. "Stop?" he half shouted. "How can I stop, Flora? How in God's name can I stop? I've lost a great deal of money. A great deal of money! Look! Look at this."

He pointed to the big sign over the machine. "Special jackpot $8,000," it read.

"See that?" he said. "When it pays off, you make eight thousand dollars!" He turned to the machine again, speaking more to it than to his wife. "Well, it's got to pay off. If a person stands here long enough, it *must* pay off."

As if to emphasize the logic of his remark, he slammed another silver dollar in the slot, pulled down the lever and stared intently at the tumblers as a cherry came up with two lemons and three silver dollars dropped into the receptacle. Again he lost himself with the machine and became oblivious to Flora. He lost five more silver dollars and felt the gnawing bite of irritation that comes with defeat.

"Franklin, darling," Flora began, "You know how awful you feel in the morning when you've been up too late at night—"

He whirled around at her and screamed, "Flora, why don't you shut your mouth."

She drew back, white-faced, feeling the shriveling shame that was always caused by Franklin's temper. He noticed it and it egged him on. It always gave him a kind of perverse satisfaction to yell at Flora. She was so plain and so weak; she was such a piece of dough to be pulled and kneaded and pounded. And she was worth screaming at, because she would react. Not like the machine that had been his enemy for so many hours, his tormentor. He wanted to kick the machine, to scratch it, gouge it, make it feel pain. But the machine was impassive and invulnerable. Flora wasn't. Flora with her mousy little face. For a passing, exploding moment he wanted to hit her, to smash his fist into her face. But it was almost as good to scream at her and get a reaction.

"I hate a shrew, Flora," he shouted.

Several people turned to stare at them.

"I can't stand a woman who hangs over your shoulder and sees to it that you have miserable luck."

He heard her sobbing intake of breath and it poured kerosene on the fire that flared inside of him.

"That's what you're doing to me now, Flora—you're

giving me miserable luck. You and your Las Vegas. You and your God-damned contests. Get out of my sight, will you? Will you get out of my sight now!"

She made one more weak, pitiful protest, "Franklin, please, people are watching—"

"The hell with people," he shouted. "I'm not concerned with people. People can go to hell."

He turned and with sweaty palms, clutched at the sides of the machine, his lips compressed. Burning on his face was the anger of frustration, mixed with the high fever of the bad gambler.

"This is what I'm concerned with," he said. "This machine! This damned machine." His anger burned hotter, his frustration took over. He pounded his knuckles against it. "It's inhuman the way it lets you win a little and then takes it all back. It teases you. It holds out promises and wheedles you. It sucks you in. And then—" He slammed another silver dollar into the slot, pulled down the lever with both hands, then watched as two plums and a lemon showed up on the tumbler and there was the dull click once again, with silence following it.

He was unaware of Flora now, unaware of the people who stood watching him behind her. He was unconscious of the noises, the lights, the sweat on his body, the fact that his mouth twitched. There was this machine in front of him. There was this machine that had a face on it and it had been cheating him and he had to pay it back. He had to revenge himself on it and the only weapons he could use were silver dollars. He put them in, pulled down the lever, watched, listened, waited.

He didn't see Flora, handkerchief to face, walk away from the machine and disappear out the door. He didn't hear a man in a cashmere sport-coat comment loudly to his wife that, "the little prune-faced guy was a real nut with that machine." A waiter asked him if he wanted a drink and he didn't look at the waiter or answer him. There were only two things left in Franklin Gibbs's world. Himself and the machine. Everything else had ceased to exist.

He was a sour-faced little man in an old-fashioned suit and he stood at the machine gorging it with silver dollars, trying to make it vomit back at him. He was a dope addict now, in the middle of a long and protracted needle, and he never really knew, even at five in the morning, when the room was empty save for one blackjack game, one dice table still operating and himself, that in every clinical sense, he'd lost his mind.

Everything that he'd used to sustain himself through his lifetime—his willfulness, his pettiness, his self-delusions, his prejudices—he'd whipped together like a suit of armor and this is what he wore as he battled the machine on into the morning. Slip in the coin, pull down the lever. Slip in the coin, pull down the lever. Slip in the coin, pull down the lever. Keep it up. Don't stop. Don't break the routine of hand and arm and eye and ear. This was the new chronology of his life function. Sooner or later the machine would pay off. It would surrender to him. It would acknowledge his superiority by suddenly spewing out eight thousand silver dollars. This was all he thought about as he stood there, oblivious to the dawn outside, to anything except that he was alone in the world with a one-armed bandit that had a face.

When the night cashier left and yawned a good morning to his replacement, he made mention of the funny little duck by the machine who'd been there something like seven hours.

"I seen them get hooked before," he said to his replacement, then shook his head, "but never like him. Never like that buggy little guy over there!"

That was the epitaph to Franklin Gibbs's first night at Las Vegas, but only to that night. At eight-thirty in the morning, when Flora came in to find him, he was still at the machine.

Marty Lubow had a brief talk with the resident manager of the hotel about eleven in the morning. They talked in passing of a couple of public relation stunts in the offing, the nature of the ad campaign for Sammy Davis, Jr., who would start at the hotel two weeks hence, and, just before Lubow left, the manager asked him about Franklin Gibbs whom several people had mentioned. There is a grapevine of no mean proportions in the Las Vegas hotel circuit. Let a man make seven straight passes at a crap table and within five minutes the information is known all over town. Or let a movie star drop a bundle and make a scene and a gossip columnist has phoned it in within an hour. But even in a town full of characters and caricatures, there was always room for one more. And a sour-faced little man in a 1937 suit was obviously setting a new record for time spent and money lost at one silver buck machine. The manager queried Lubow as to the nature of the beast and Lubow laughingly told him that if Gibbs could hold out till six that evening they could probably set up some picture stuff. This might be a natural for *Life* magazine.

But at three o'clock that afternoon, after Lubow had seen Franklin, he was no longer interested in any kind of press coverage. Quite the contrary. One look at the little man's face was quite sufficient to have him phone the house physician to inquire somewhat obliquely how long a man could live without sleep.

At five-thirty, Franklin Gibbs had lost three thousand, eight hundred dollars, cashed three checks, downed one glass of orange juice, one half of a boiled ham sandwich, and had come close to striking his wife across the side of the face when, with tears rolling down her cheeks, she had pleaded with him to come back to the room to take a nap.

Franklin Gibbs's life was entirely funneled into the slot machine in front of him. At this point he had no recollection of ever having done anything but feed in coins and pull down levers. He felt neither thirst nor hunger. He knew he was desperately tired and that his vision seemed out of focus, but there was no question of giving up.

It wasn't until nine o'clock that evening, after the hotel manager had told him he would be unable to cash another check and Flora had telegraphed his brother in Iowa—a rambling, incoherent telegram which spoke of disaster—that Franklin Gibbs got an ice-cold, clutching feeling in his gut. He had three silver dollars left and he'd reached the point where he kept mumbling to the machine that it was now time to pay off. He was owed eight thousand silver dollars and there wasn't any question about it. What was the matter with the machine, any-way? Didn't it know the rules? He kept talking to it, urging it, arguing with it—sweaty, sodden, obsessed. It was just twenty-one minutes after eleven when Franklin Gibbs put in the last silver dollar. The machine made a strange kind of whirring noise and the lever stopped half-way down on its arc, clanked noisily and then stuck. Franklin Gibbs stood stock-still for a long, unbelieving moment and it came to him that right then, right at that instant, he was being taken. This was the moment of the big cheat. Obviously this was the coin that was to have brought him the eight-thousand-dollar jackpot. He had no doubt about it at all. He was supposed to have won this time, and the machine, the machine with the ugly face, the machine that had hounded him by calling out his name, had now stooped to the nadir of deceit and was refusing to pay off.

Franklin felt ripples of anger rise up from deep inside him, anger that began as a trickle and built to a coursing flood. Anger that bubbled and seethed and boiled. Anger that suddenly pinched at him and clutched at him and tore at him.

"What's the idea?" he shouted at the machine. "What's the idea, you bastard! Goddamn you. Give me back my dollar. That's my last one, you miserable, crummy, dirty—" His breath caught up with him and for a mo-ment all he could do was wheeze. "Give me back my Goddamned dollar."

He hit the machine. He punched it. He clawed at it. He shoved it. Two floor men, a cashier and the assistant manager, headed toward him from opposite points of the room, but not before he had broken the knuckles of his right hand and not before he had pushed the machine off its stand to go crashing down to the floor, and not before he had thrown himself on it, tangling himself up in it, cutting his arm against the broken glass that was its nose and bleeding all over the carpet.

They led him out of the room, screaming, crying, sob-bing, shouting and fighting. Flora ran after them, wring-ing her hands and weeping.

The house physician set and bandaged Franklin's hand, put three stitches in his arm and gave him a sedative. They undressed him, put him to bed, then stood over him while he fell into an uneasy sleep. The doctor told Flora that it would be best to take him home the following day and that Franklin should have a long session with his own physician when he returned to Elgin, Kansas. He even murmured something about the possibility of psychiatric help later on. Flora kept nodding at him, her face pale and tear-stained. After they had gone she sat silently staring at her husband.

Somewhere in the nether land of Franklin Gibbs's subconscious he heard a voice clear and distinct. It was produced by coins rubbing against themselves. It was a metallic, clanking, "Franklin!" that suddenly was shouted into the air. He woke with a start and heard it again. Then again. He got out of bed and walked past a frightened Flora toward the door.

"Franklin!" It came from the hall outside. It mocked him. It assailed him. It spit at him. He flung open the door. There was the machine in the corridor, its eyes blinking on and off.

"Franklin," it cajoled him. "Franklin, Franklin, Franklin."

He screamed and slammed the door.

"Franklin, Franklin, Franklin."

The noise of it filled the room and then he saw it staring at him in the bedroom mirror. He screamed again and turning, saw it behind the chair. He backed against the closet door and mistaking it for an escape route, flung it open. There was the machine inside the closet blinking at him and calling his name. He tripped and sprawled on the floor, banging his head against the corner of the dresser, and there was the machine looking at him from the center of the room.

"Franklin, Franklin, Franklin," it called out to him.

He couldn't scream any more. He had no voice left. All he had to clutch was his terror. A silent, voiceless terror. He scrambled to his feet and ran this way and that way, now bumping against furniture, now falling into the arms of Flora who scrabbled at him, shouting his name. He opened the door to the hall and there was the machine grinning at him.

The last moment of Franklin Gibbs's life was spent in a mad dash across the hotel room toward the window. He went through it, taking most of the glass with him, to land two stories below on the concrete walk that surrounded the big swimming pool. He hit it, forehead first, and the loud snap that separated his vertebrae at the back of his neck bore no relationship to any sound that Flora had ever heard before. But she heard this over the sound of her own screaming as she stood at the broken window and looked down at the crumpled figure of Franklin Gibbs in his pajamas, his head tilted at an odd angle to his body. He was quite dead.

No one was allowed to touch the body. Someone had tastefully and compassionately covered it with a blanket. A sheriff's deputy had phoned for the ambulance and was just now succeeding in getting most of the people out of the pool area.

Mr. Lubow, white-faced with anxiety, was in Flora's room helping her pack. He was telling her there was a much more comfortable little sanitarium at the other end of the town and he was quite certain she'd be able to rest there much more easily. She sat on the edge of the bed while he talked to her in low, nervous gusts about how sad and sorry they were that this had happened. She was a dough-faced, catatonic sphinx whose life had suddenly drained away. She had a vague passing thought that she should telegraph Franklin's brother again and she thought additionally that Franklin hadn't believed in insurance, but both thoughts were dulled and stifled by a blanket of neutral dullness that she let settle over her. She didn't want to think any more. She was too tired.

Down by the pool Franklin Gibbs's body lay cold and broken. One lifeless hand extended from underneath the blanket, resting on the concrete. In the dark shrubbery beyond, there was a rattle of noise. A silver dollar fell to the ground and rolled unerringly across the walk to spin to a stop right next to Franklin Gibbs's hand.

No one in the hotel could explain what the one-armed

bandit was doing near the pool where they found it the following morning. It was in pretty bad shape, dented, scratched, with the lever stuck tight and most of its glass broken, but they sent it to the factory for a repair job and it was due back on the line within a week or two. The pool boy found the silver dollar also the following morning and put it in his pocket and Flora Gibbs flew back to Elgin, Kansas, to pick up the broken crockery of her life.

She lived a silent, patient life from then on and gave no one any trouble. Only once did anything unusual happen and that was a year later. The church had a bazaar and someone brought in an old used one-armed bandit. It had taken three of her friends from the Women's Alliance to stop her screaming and get her back home to bed. It had cast rather a pall over the evening.

From Rod Serling's closing narration, "The Fever," The Twilight Zone, February 5, 1960, CBS Television Network.

NARRATOR'S VOICE

Mr. Franklin Gibbs, visitor to Las Vegas,
who lost his money, his reason, and
finally his life to an inanimate metal
machine variously described as—a one-
armed bandit, a slot machine or, in
Mr. Franklin Gibbs's words, a monster
with a will all its own. For our
purposes we'll stick with the latter
because we're in The Twilight Zone!

FADE TO BLACK

Where Is Everybody?

The sensation was unrelated to anything he'd ever felt before. He awoke, but had no recollection of ever having gone to sleep. And, to mystify him further, he was not in a bed. He was walking down a road, a two-lane black macadam with a vivid white stripe running down the center. He stopped, stared up at a blue sky, a hot, mid-morning sun. Then he looked around at a rural landscape, high, full-leafed trees flanking the road. Beyond the trees were fields of wheat, golden and rippling.

Like Ohio, he thought. Or maybe Indiana. Or parts of upstate New York. Suddenly he was conscious of the words being thought. Ohio. Indiana. New York. It immediately occurred to him that he didn't know where he was. A new thought followed quickly—he didn't know *who* he was, either! He looked down at himself, fingering the green, one-piece set of coveralls he was wearing, the heavy, high shoes, the zippered front that went from neck to crotch. He touched his face and then his hair. An inventory. Trying to piece together items of familiarity. An orientation through the tips of his fingers. He felt a light beard stubble, a nose slightly indented at the bridge, moderately heavy eyebrows, close-cropped hair. Not quite a butch—but close. He was young. Reasonably young, anyway. And he felt good. Healthy. At peace. He was confused as hell, but not at all frightened.

He walked over to the side of the road, took out a cigarette and lit it. He stood there leaning in the shade of one of the giant oaks that flanked the road. And he thought: I don't know who I am. I don't know where I am. But it's summer and I'm out in the country some place and this must be some kind of amnesia or something.

He drew deeply and enjoyably on the cigarette. As he took it out of his mouth and held it between his fingers, he looked at it. King-sized and filtered. Phrases came to him. "Winstons taste good like a cigarette should." "You get a lot to like in a Marlboro." "Are you smoking more now but enjoying it less?" That was for Camels —the kind you used to be willing to walk a mile for. He grinned and then laughed out loud. The power of advertising. He could stand there not knowing his name or where he was, but the twentieth-century poetry of the tobacco company cut across even the boundaries of amnesia. He stopped laughing and considered. Cigarettes and slogans meant America. So that's what he was—an American.

He flipped away the cigarette and walked on. A few hundred yards up the road he heard music coming from around the bend ahead. Loud trumpets. Good ones. There was a drum in the background and then a single, high-flying trumpet that rode an obbligato to the percussion. Swing. That's what it was, and again he was conscious of a word symbol that meant something to him. Swing. And this one he could relate to a specific time. It went with the 1930s. And this was beyond the thirties. This was the fifties. The 1950s. He let these facts pile up on top of one another. He felt like the key piece of a jigsaw puzzle, other pieces falling into place around him, forming a recognizable picture. And it was odd, he thought, how definite the pattern was, once they fell. Now he knew it was 1959. This was beyond doubt. Nineteen fifty-nine.

As he rounded the bend and saw the source of the music, he took a quick inventory of what he had discovered. He was an American, maybe in his twenties, it was summer, and here he was.

In front of him was a diner, a small, rectangular clapboard building with a sign on the front door which read, "OPEN." Music was pouring out the front door. He went inside and got an impression of familiarity. He'd been to places like this before, this much he knew definitely. A long counter studded with catsup bottles and napkin holders; a back wall plastered with hand-written signs announcing kinds of sandwiches, soups, pie a la mode, and a dozen other items. There were a couple of large posters with girls in bathing suits holding up Coke bottles, and at the far end of the room was what he knew to be a juke box, the source of the music.

He walked the length of the counter, swinging a couple of seats around as he passed. Behind the counter an open swinging door led to the kitchen where he could see a big restaurant stove, a pot of coffee perking on it. The gurgling sound of the coffee was familiar and comforting and sent an aroma of breakfast and morning into the room.

The young man smiled as if seeing an old friend, or better, *feeling* the presence of an old friend. He sat down on the last stool so that he could see into the kitchen. There were shelves laden with canned goods, a big double-door refrigerator, a wooden chopping table, a screen door. He looked up at the signs on the wall. The Denver sandwich. The hamburger. Cheeseburger. Ham and eggs. Again he was aware of the phenomenon of having to associate obviously familiar words with what they represented. What was a Denver sandwich, for example? And what was pie a la mode? Then, after a few moments of reflection, a picture came into his mind along with a taste. He had an odd thought then, that he was like an infant who was being exposed to the maturing process in a fantastically telescoped, jet-propelled way.

The music on the juke box broke through his thoughts, loud and intrusive.

He called out, toward the kitchen, "That loud enough for you, is it?"

There was a silence. Only the music answered him.

He raised his voice, "Can you hear it okay?"

Still no response. He went over to the machine, pushed it out a few inches from the wall and found a small volume-knob near the base. He turned it. The music fell away from him and the room seemed quieter and more comfortable. He pushed the machine back against the wall and returned to his stool. He picked up the cardboard menu that was leaning against the napkin-holder and studied it, occasionally looking up into the kitchen. He could see four pies browning nicely through the glass door of the oven and again there was the sense of something familiar, something friendly that he could respond to.

He called out again: "I think I'll have ham and eggs. Eggs up and easy and some hash browns."

Still there was no movement from the kitchen and no answering voice.

"I saw a sign that there was a town up ahead. What's the name of it?"

Coffee bubbled in the big enamelled pot, the steam rising into the air. A light wind moved the screen door in a creaking four-inch arc back and forth, and the juke box continued to play quietly. The young man was getting hungry now and felt a little nudge of irritation.

"Hey," he called out, "I asked you a question in there. What's the name of the town up ahead?"

He waited for a moment and when there was no answer he got up from the stool, vaulted the counter, pushed the swinging door open and went into the kitchen. It was empty. He walked through to the screen door, pulled it open and went outside. There was a big gravel back yard, unpunctuated by anything but a row of garbage cans, one of which had tipped over, littering the ground with a collection of tin cans, coffee grounds, egg shells and some empty cereal boxes; some orange crates; a broken, partially spokeless wheel; three or four piles of old newspapers. He was about to go back inside when something made him stop dead. He looked again at the garbage cans. There was something missing. An element not there that should have been there. He didn't know what it was. It was just a minute tilt to the dial inside his head that registered balance and reason. Something was wrong and he didn't know what it was. It left him with a tiny feeling of disquiet which he pushed into the back of his mind.

He returned to the kitchen, went over to the coffeepot,

smelled it again, carried it over to the chopping table. He found a mug and poured himself a cup of hot coffee. He leaned against the back of the chopping table and sipped the coffee, enjoying it, liking its familiarity.

Then he went into the other room and took a large doughnut from a glass jar. He carried it back to the kitchen, and leaned against the jamb of the swinging door so that he could survey both rooms. He munched slowly on the doughnut, sipped at the coffee, and reflected. Whoever ran this place, he thought, is either in the basement or maybe his wife's having a baby. Or maybe the guy's sick. Maybe he's had a coronary or something. Maybe he should look around and find a basement door. He looked over at the cash register behind the counter. What an easy set up for a heist. Or for a free meal. Or for anything, for that matter.

The young man reached in his pocket and pulled out a handful of coins and a dollar bill.

"American money," he said aloud. "That settles that. No question about it. I *am* an American. Two half-dollars. A quarter. A dime. Four pennies and a dollar bill. That's American money."

He went into the kitchen again, looking up at the cereal boxes with the familiar names. The Campbell soup cans. Was that the one with the fifty-seven varieties? Again he reflected on who he was and where he was. On the disjointed *non sequiturs* that passed through his consciousness; his knowledge of music, the colloquialisms he spoke, the menu that he read and understood perfectly. Ham and eggs and hash browns—things he could relate to appearance and taste and smell. And then a phalanx of questions marched by. Exactly who was he? What the hell was he doing there? And where was "there"? And why? That was the *big* question. Why did he suddenly wake up on a road and not know who he was? And why wasn't anyone in the diner? Where was the owner or the cook or the counterman? Why weren't they there? And again the little germ of disquiet that he'd felt outside stirred inside him.

He chewed the last piece of doughnut, swigged it down with what remained of the coffee, and went back into the other room. Once again he vaulted over the counter; tossed a quarter on top of it. At the front door, he turned and surveyed the room again. Damn it, but it was normal, it was real, it was natural looking. The words, the place, the smell, the look. He put his hand on the knob of the door and pulled it open. He was about to step outside when a thought hit him. Suddenly he knew what had disturbed him about the garbage cans. He carried this disquiet with him as he walked out into the hot morning.

He knew what was the missing element and the knowledge gave him a cold, apprehension that he hadn't felt before. It did little jarring things to his nerve endings because suddenly something formed and entered into his thoughts. Something that couldn't be understood. Something beyond the norm. Beyond the word symbols, past the realm of logic that had been supporting him and answering his questions and giving him a link to reality.

There were no flies.

He walked around the corner of the building to stare again at the back yard with its row of garbage cans. There were no flies. There was a silence and nothing stirred and there were no flies.

He walked slowly back toward the highway, suddenly conscious of what was wrong. The trees were real and the highway and the diner with everything in it. The smell of the coffee was real and the taste of the doughnut and the cereals had the right names and Coca Cola came in a bottle and cost a nickel. It was all right and proper and everything was in its right place. *But there was no life to it!* This was the missing element—activity! This was the thought he carried down the highway past a sign which said, "Carsville, 1 mile."

He entered the town and it spread out in front of him, neat and attractive. A small main street circled a village park that lay in the center of everything. Set back in the middle of this park area was a large school. On the circular main street were a row of stores, a movie theater, more stores and a police station. Further down was a church, a residential street that lay beyond and finally a drugstore on the corner. There was a book store, a confectionery, a grocery store and out in front of it, a small sign which read "Bus Stop." It lay there quietly and prettily in the mid-morning sun and it was quiet. There was no sound at all.

He walked down the sidewalk peering into the windows. All of the stores were open. The bakery had fresh cake and cookies. The book store was running a special sale. The movie theater advertised a picture out front having to do with war in the air. There was a three-story office building that told of lawyers inside, public notary and a real estate firm. Further down there was a glass-enclosed public telephone and then a department store with a delivery entrance blocked off from the street by a wire mesh fence.

Once again he reflected on the phenomena. There were the stores, the park, the bus stop, the whole works, but there were no people. There wasn't a soul to be seen. He leaned against the side of the bank building and scanned the street left to right, as if somehow he could find something stirring if he looked hard enough.

It was when his eyes reached the fence fronting the department store delivery entrance directly across the street, that he saw the girl. She was sitting in a truck parked inside the yard, plain as day—the very first person he'd seen. He felt his heart jump as he nervously stepped off the curb and started walking toward her. Halfway across the street he stopped, feeling his palms wet. He had an impulse to run like hell over to the truck or to stand there and shout questions at the girl. He forced a matter-of-factness into his tone, made himself smile.

"Hey, Miss! Miss, over here." He felt his voice rising higher and again he made an effort to keep it low and conversational. "Miss, I wonder if you could help me. I was wondering if you knew where everyone was. Doesn't seem to be anyone around. Literally . . . not a soul."

Now he took what he hoped was a sauntering walk across the street toward her, noticing that she continued to look straight at him from inside the cab of the truck. He reached the other side of the street, stopped a few feet from the wire mesh gate and smiled at her again.

"It's a crazy thing," he said. "Crazy, odd-ball thing.

When I woke up this morning—" He stopped and he thought this over. "Well, I didn't exactly wake up," he said. "I just sort of—just sort of found myself walking down the road."

He reached the sidewalk, went through the half-open gate to the passenger side of the truck. The girl inside wasn't looking at him any longer. She was staring straight out through the front windshield and he saw her profile. Beautiful woman. Long blonde hair. But pale. He tried to think where he'd seen features like that—so immobile, so without expression. Bland, yes, but more than bland. Spiritless.

"Look, Miss," he said, "I don't want to frighten you, but there must be somebody around here who could tell me—"

His hand had opened the truck door when his voice was cut off by the girl's body as she slumped over, past the wide, amazed eyes of the young man, and down, hitting the sidewalk with a loud, almost metallic clank. He stared down at the upturned face, then became aware of words on the panel of the truck, "Resnick's Store Mannequins." He looked back at her face—the wooden, lifeless face with the painted cheeks and the painted mouth and the fixed half-smile, with the eyes that were wide open and showed nothing, told nothing. Eyes that looked exactly what they were—holes in a dummy's face. Something of the humor of it struck him now. He grinned, scratched his jaw, then slowly slid down, his back against the side of the truck till he was sitting next to the mannequin who lay there staring up at the blue sky and the hot sun.

The young man nudged her hard wooden arm, winked, clucked his tongue and said, "You'll forgive me, babe, but at no time did I mean to be so upsetting. As a matter of fact"—he nudged her again—"I've always had kind of a secret yen for the quiet type." Now he reached over to pinch the unyielding cheek and laughed again. "Get what I mean, babe?"

He picked up the dummy, and carefully deposited her back in the cab of the truck, pulling her dress down to a modest point over the knees. He closed the cab door, then turned and took a few aimless steps away from the truck. On the other side of the mesh gate was the circular main street with the small park in the middle. He went to the fence and let his eyes move left to right once more, taking in every one of the stores, as if by some unique concentration he might find a sign of life. But the street lay empty, the stores were unoccupied, the silence was persistent.

He went toward the service entrance of the department store beyond the truck, stuck his head into a dark hall, loaded with mannequins piled nude on top of one another. The thought hit him that it was like World War II pictures of the gas ovens at the concentration camps, the way they were piled on top of one another. He was disturbed by the similarity and hurriedly backed out into the delivery yard. Then he shouted toward the open door.

"Hey! Anybody here? Anybody hear me?"

He went to the truck again and looked inside. There was no key in the ignition. He grinned at the lifeless face of the mannequin.

"How about it, babe? You wouldn't know where the ignition keys would be, would you?"

The mannequin stared straight ahead at the windshield.

It was then he heard the sound. The first he'd heard outside the diner. At first it made no sense to him. It was unrelated to anything he knew or could associate with the stillness. Then he realized what the sound was. It was a phone ringing. He ran toward the fence, slamming himself against it, his fingers gripping the wire strands, his eyes darting around until he found what he was looking for. It was the glass enclosed public phone booth just across the street, a few yards into the park. The phone was still ringing.

The young man flung himself through the gate and raced across the street. He reached the booth at a dead run, flung open the glass door and almost pulled the phone out by the wire as he grabbed the receiver off the hook. He kicked the door shut behind him.

"Hello. Hello!" He jangled the receiver furiously. "Hello! Operator? Operator?"

The phone was dead. He waited a moment, then

slammed the receiver back on the cradle. He reached into his breast pocket and pulled out a dime. He shoved it in the slot and waited. Presently he heard his first voice, the colorless, astringently courteous tone of a telephone operator.

"The number you have reached," the voice said, "is not a working number—"

The young man was angry now. He shouted into the phone. "Are you out of your minds down there? I didn't dial a number—"

"Please be sure you have the right number and are dialing it correctly."

"I didn't dial a number, operator. The phone rang and I answered it." Again he jiggled the hook wildly. "Operator. Operator, will you listen to me, please? All I want to know is where I am. Understand? I just want to find out where I am and where the people are. Please, operator, listen—"

Again the operator's voice, impersonal, cold, as if from another planet. "The number you have reached is not a working number. Please make sure you have the right number and are dialing it correctly."

Then there was a long pause before the voice continued, "This is a recording!"

The young man slowly replaced the receiver and stood there conscious now of the quiet town that surrounded him through the glass, terribly aware of the silence that hung over the place, a silence punctuated by what the operator had said. "This is a recording." The whole damn place was a recording. Sound put on wax. Pictures put on canvas. Things placed on a stage. But only for effect. But a voice—that was a lousy joke.

The inanimate things such as unattended coffeepots, mannequins, stores—these he could wonder at and walk away. But a human voice—he desperately needed to know that this was surrounded with flesh and blood. It was a cheat to have it any other way. It was a promise and then a withdrawal. It made him angry in addition to causing that tiny flutter of frightened concern. The phone book was hanging by a chain. He grabbed it, ripped it open, started to read through the pages. The names sprang up at him. Abel. Baker. Botsford. Carstairs. Cathers. Cepeda.

"Well, where are you people," he shouted. "Where do you hang out? Where do you live? Just in this Goddamned book here?"

Again he riffled through the pages. The Dempseys. The Farvers. The Grannigans. And so on to a man named Zatelli who lived on North Front Street and whose first initial was A. The young man let the book drop from his hands. It swung back and forth on the chain. Slowly his head lifted until he stared out at the empty street.

"Look, boys," he said softly. "Who's watching the stores?" The glass windows looked back at him. *"Who's watching any of the stores?"*

He turned slowly, put his hand on the door and pushed. The door remained stationary. He pushed again. It was stuck tight. And now he had the feeling that it was a gag. A very big, complex, terribly unfunny gag. He pushed hard, throwing his shoulder against the door and still it did not move.

"Awright," he shouted. "Awright, it's a very funny joke. Very funny. I love your town. I love the sense of humor. But now it's not funny any more. Understand? Now it stinks. Who's the wise guy who locked me in here?" Now he kicked, shoved, pushed at the door until the sweat rolled down his face. He closed his eyes and leaned against the glass for a moment and then suddenly looked down to see the door hinge arched toward him. He gently pulled and the door swung open, bent and out of alignment, but open. He'd been pushing on it instead of pulling. It was as simple as that. He felt he should laugh or perhaps apologize to something or someone, but of course, there was no one to apologize to.

He stepped out into the sunlight and went across the park toward a building with a big glass globe in front with lettering on it which read "Police." He smiled to himself as he went toward it. Head for law and order, he thought. But more than just law and order—head for sanity. Maybe that's where to find it. When you're a little boy and lost, your mother tells you to go up to the nice policeman and tell him your name. Well, now he was a little boy and he was lost and there was no one else he could report to. And as to a name—someone would have to tell *him*.

The police station was dark and cool, split in half by a counter which ran the length of the room. Behind it was the sergeant's desk and chair and across the far wall a radio operator's table with microphone and a CW sending and receiving set. To the right was a barred door into a cell block. He went through the swinging door in the middle of the counter to the microphone. He picked it up, studying it, then illogically, as if it were expected of him to go along with the gag, he put on an official radio-car voice.

"Calling all cars. Calling all cars. Unknown man walking around police station. Very suspicious-looking egg. Probably wants to—"

His voice broke off. Across the room by the sergeant's desk, a thin column of smoke drifted lazily up toward the ceiling. He slowly put down the microphone and went to the desk. A big, quarter-smoked cigar was lying in an ash tray, lighted and smoking. He picked it up, then put it down. He felt a tension, a fear, a sense of being watched and listened to. He whirled around as if to catch someone in the act of just that—staring and listening.

The room was empty. He opened the barred door. It creaked noisily. He went into the cell block. There were eight cells, four on each side, and they were all empty. Through the bars of the last cell on the right he could see a sink. Water was running. Hot water. He saw the steam. On a shelf was a razor, dripping wet and a shaving brush, full of lather. He closed his eyes for a moment because this was too much. This was far too much. Show me goblins, he thought, or ghosts or monsters. Show me dead people walking in a parade. Play shrill and discordant trumpet sounds on a funeral horn that jars the stillness of the morning—but stop frightening me with the grotesque normality of things. Don't show me cigar butts in ash trays and water running in a sink and lather-covered shaving brushes. These are what shock more than apparitions.

He slowly entered the cell and went to the sink. He

reached out a trembling hand and touched the lather on the brush. It was real. It felt warm. It smelled of soap. The water dripped into the sink. The razor said Gillette, and he thought of the World Series on television and the New York Giants taking four in a row from the Cleveland Indians. But God that must have been ten years ago. Or maybe it was last year. Or maybe it hadn't happened yet. Because now he had no base, no starting point, no date or time or place of reference. He was not conscious of the sound of the creaking cell door, as it slowly closed on him, until he saw the shadow of it on the wall inching across slowly, inexorably.

He let out a sob and flung himself across to the door, squeezing through just before it closed. He hung on to it for a moment, then backed away from the cell to lean against the door on the opposite side, and stare across at the now closed and locked door as if it were a kind of poisonous animal.

Something told him to run. Run. Run like hell. Get out. Take off. Get away. It was a whispered command in his inner ear. It was a last ditch order from an embattled mind, assaulted by nightmarish fear that could at any moment lock him rooted to the earth. It was all his instincts screaming at him in the name of safety and salvation. Get the hell out of here. Run! Run! *RUN!*

He was outside in the sun racing across the street, stumbling over the curb, scratching himself on a hedge as he ploughed head first into it. Then over the hedge and into the park, running, running, running. He saw the school building loom up in front of him and there was a statue in front. His motion carried him up the steps to the statue until suddenly he found himself clutching a metal leg of a heroic looking educator who died in 1911 and whose metal visage loomed up in front of him silhouetted against the blue sky. Then he began to cry. He looked up at the stillness, the stores, the movie theater, and finally the statue, and he cried. "Where is everybody? Please, for Christ's sake tell me . . . where is everybody?"

The young man sat on the curb in the late afternoon

staring down at his shadow and the other shadows that flanked him. A store awning, a bus-stop sign, a streetlight post—formless globs of shadow that stretched across the sidewalk in a line. He slowly rose to his feet, looked briefly at the bus-stop sign and then down the street as if in some half-hearted, half-hopeless expectation of seeing a big red and white bus approach, open its doors, let out a crowd of people. People. That's what the young man wanted to see. His own kind.

The silence had been building all day. It had become an entity all of itself, a pressure on him, an oppressive, hot, itchy, wool-like thing that surrounded and covered him, that made him sweat and squirm and wish he could throw it off and crawl out.

He took a slow walk down the main street—his fortieth or fiftieth walk down that same street since morning. He passed the now familiar stores, looking into the now familiar doors, and it was the same. Counters, goods unattended.

He entered a bank for the fourth time that afternoon, and also for the fourth time, walked behind the tellers' cages, picking up handfuls of money and throwing them aside. Once he lit his cigarette from a hundred-dollar bill and laughed uproariously at it until suddenly, after he'd thrown the half-burnt bill down on the ground, he found himself unable to laugh any longer. All right, so a guy can light a cigarette from a hundred-dollar bill—but so what?

He walked out of the bank and then crossed the street and headed for the drugstore. There was a two-for-one sale announced on signs plastered across the window. Church bells rang from down the street and this jarred him. For a moment he flattened himself against the side of the drugstore staring wildly toward the sound until he realized what it was.

He walked into the drugstore, a big, square room surrounded by high counters and shelves with many glass display cases running in lines across the room. A big, mirror-backed fountain was at the rear, with pictures of floats and frappes and sodas and malts. He stopped by the cigar counter, helped himself to an expensive one, took off its paper and sniffed.

"A good cigar, that's what this country needs," he said aloud as he walked toward the fountain. "A good cigar. A couple of good cigars. And some people to smoke them."

He put the cigar carefully in a breast pocket and went in back of the fountain. From there he scanned the room, the empty booths, the juke box selectors over each one. And felt the stillness of the place that was totally incongruous with what was in it. It was a room poised for action; a room on the verge of coming alive, but never quite doing so. Behind the fountain were the ice-cream containers. He picked up an ice-cream scoop, took a glass dish from a shelf near the mirror and put two large scoops of ice cream in it. He covered this with syrup, then with nuts, added a cherry and some whipped cream.

He looked up and said, "How about it, anybody? Anybody for a sundae?" He paused and listened to the silence. "Nobody, huh? Okay."

He spooned up a large hunk of ice cream and cherry and whipped cream, put it in his mouth and liked the taste of it. For the first time he saw his reflection in the mirror and he was not surprised by what he saw. The face had a vaguely familiar look, not handsome, but not unpleasant. And young, he thought. It was quite young. It was the face of a man well under thirty. Maybe twenty-five or twenty-six, but no older. He studied the reflection. "You'll forgive me, old pal," he said to it, "but I don't recollect the name. The face seems familiar, but the name escapes me."

He took another bite of the ice cream, rolled it around in his mouth, melted it, and swallowed it, watching these actions in the mirror. He pointed the spoon very casually at the image.

"I'll tell you what my problem is. I'm in the middle of a nightmare that I can't wake up from. You're part of it. You and the ice cream and the cigar. The police station and the phone booth—that little mannequin." He looked down at the ice cream and then around at the drugstore then back to his reflection.

"This whole bloody town—wherever it is—*whatever*

it is—" He cocked his head to one side, suddenly remembering something and he grinned at the image.

"I just remembered something. Scrooge said it. You remember Scrooge, old buddy—Ebenezer Scrooge? It's what he said to the ghost, Jacob Marley. He said, 'You may be an undigested bit of beef, a blot of mustard. A crumb of cheese. A fragment of an undone potato. But there's more of gravy about you than grave.'"

He put the spoon down now and pushed the ice cream away. "You see? That's what you are. That's what you all are. You're what I had for dinner last night." Now the smile faded. Something intense crept into the voice. "But I've had it now. I've had it. I want to wake up." He turned from the mirror to the store and the empty booths. "If I can't wake up I've got to find somebody to talk to. That much I've *got* to do. I've got to find somebody to talk to."

For the first time he noticed a card standing on the counter. It was a basketball schedule of Carsville High School, announcing that on September 15th Carsville would play Corinth High. On September 21st, Carsville would play Leedsville. There'd be games on through December with six or seven other high schools—this was all announced matter-of-factly, quite officially, on the large poster.

"I must be a very imaginative guy," the young man said at last. "Very, very imaginative. Everything right down to the last detail. The last little detail."

He left the fountain and crossed the room to where there were several revolving pocket-book racks. Titles on the book covers flicked briefly across his consciousness, then disappeared. Murder stories, introduced on the covers by blondes in negligees, with titles like *The Brothel Death Watch*. Reprints of famous novels and gag books. Something called *Utterly Mad,* with a smiling half-wit face, captioned, "Alfred E. Neuman says, 'What, me worry!'" Some of the books seemed familiar. Fragments of plots and characters made brief excursions into his mind. He absent-mindedly turned the racks as he walked by. They creaked around, sending titles, pictures and covers

blurring in front of his eyes, until he saw one that made
him reach forward, grab the rack to stop it.

The book's cover depicted a kind of vast desert with a
tiny, almost undistinguishable figure of a human being
standing in the middle of it, arms akimbo, staring up toward the sky. There was a dim range of mountains beyond and, seemingly rising from the mountaintops, was a
single line title, *The Last Man On Earth.*

The young man riveted his eyes to these words, feeling a fusion taking place between mind and sight. *The
Last Man On Earth.* There was something especially mean-
ingful—something of particular significance—something
that suddenly made him gasp and whirl the rack around,
sending the title off into a blurred orbit.

But when the rack slowed down, the book cover took
on clarity again and it was then that he discovered there
were many of them. There were many books of the last
man on earth. Row after row of tiny figures standing,
arms outstretched, on vast deserts, each cover staring
back at him as the rack slowed and finally stopped moving.

He backed away from the books, unable to take his
eyes away from them, until he reached the front door
and briefly saw his reflection in the mirror—a white-
faced, youngish looking man who stood at the entrance
to a drugstore, looking tired, lonely, desperate and—
frightened.

He went out, assuming composure while both his body
and his mind pulled and yanked at him. Halfway across
the street, he stopped, turning round and round and round.
Suddenly he shouted, "Hey? Hey! Hey, anybody? Anybody see me? Anybody hear me? Hey!"

An answer came after a moment. The deep throated,
melodic bells of the church pealed out the notice of the
passing day. They rang five times and then stopped. The
echo lingered, and then this too faded away. The young
man went down the street past the now familiar stores,
no longer seeing them. His eyes were open but he saw
nothing. He kept thinking of the book titles—*The Last
Man On Earth,* and it did something to his insides. It was

as if a heavy glob of indigestible food had gone protesting down his throat to settle, leaden and heavy, in his gut. *The Last Man On Earth.* The picture and the words stuck with frightening clarity in his consciousness. The tiny figure of the lone man in the desert, hands outstretched. The indistinct, lonely little figure whose fate was spread across the sky, across the mountain ranges beyond it—the last man on earth. He couldn't shake that picture or the words, as he headed toward the park.

He was quite unaware that the afternoon sun now looked pale and distant as it moved across the sky. It was on its way out for that day.

It was night and the young man sat on a park bench close to the statue in front of the school. He played tic-tac-toe with a stick in the dirt, winning game after game and then wiping out each victory with the heel of his shoe to begin all over again. He'd made himself a sandwich in a small restaurant. He'd walked through the department store and then through a Woolworth five-and-dime. He'd gone into the school, through empty classrooms and had stifled an impulse to scrawl obscenities on a blackboard. Anything to shock or jar or to defy. Anything in the way of a gesture to rip away at the façade of reality that surrounded him. He was sure it was a façade. He was sure it must be just the real quality of the unreal dream and if only he could erase it and reveal what was underneath!—but he couldn't.

A light shone on his hand. He looked up startled. Street lights were going on and lights in the park joined them. Light after light all over the town. Street lights. Store windows. And then the flickering of the marquee lights in front of the theater.

He rose from the bench and went to the theater and stopped by the tiny box office. A ticket was sticking out of the metal slot. He put it in his breast pocket and was about to go inside when he saw a poster announcing the movie inside. On the poster was a large blow-up of an air force pilot, profile to the sky, staring up at a flight of jet aircraft that streaked across and over him.

The young man took a step toward the poster. Slowly

and unconsciously his hands touched the coveralls he was wearing and very gradually there was a bridge between himself and the man on the poster. And then it came to him. They were dressed alike. The coveralls were almost identical. The young man grew excited, and some of the fatigue washed away, leaving behind it an enthusiasm bordering on exultation. He reached out and touched the poster. Then he whirled around to look toward the empty streets and spoke aloud.

"I'm Air Force. That's it. I'm Air Force. I'm in the Air Force. That's right! I remember. I'm in the Air Force." It was a tiny, insignificant skein to a crazy quilt blanket of unknowns—but it *was* something he could pick up and hold and analyze. It *was* a clue. And it was the first one. The only one.

"I'm in the Air Force," he shouted. He headed into the theater. "I'm in the Air Force!" His voice reverberated through the empty lobby. "Hey, anybody, everybody, somebody—I'm in the Air Force!" He yelled it into the theater, the words banging through the air, over the row after row of empty seats and hitting against the huge, white, motionless screen at the far end.

The young man sat down and found he was perspiring. He felt for a handkerchief, pulled it out, wiped his face. He felt the beard stubble, knowing that there were a thousand closed doors to his subconscious that he was close to opening.

"Air Force," he said softly now. "Air Force. But what does that mean? What does 'Air Force' mean?" His head jerked upward. "Was there a bomb? Is that it? That *must* have been it. A bomb—" He stopped, shaking his head. "But if there'd been a bomb, everything would have been destroyed. And nothing's been destroyed. How could it have been a—"

The lights began to dim and a strong beam of light from a projectionist's booth somewhere in the rear of the theater suddenly shone on the white screen. There was the sound of music, loud, blaring, martial music, and on the screen a B-52 bomber headed down a runway and suddenly screamed into the air over his head. There were more big B-52's and now they were in the sky, a flight of them, heading up leaving lines of vapor trails. And always the music blaring out underneath it.

The young man rose to his feet, his eyes wide, disbelieving. The beam of light disappeared into a small, blinking hole high above a balcony.

"Hey!" he screamed. "Who's showing the picture? Somebody must be showing the picture! Hey! Do you see me? I'm down here. Hey, whoever's showing the picture— I'm down here!"

He ran up the aisle, through the lobby, and up the stairs to the balcony. He stumbled across the dark seats, falling several times and finally, not finding an aisle, he simply crawled and jumped and scrambled over the tops of seats toward the small bright hole in the wall at the far end. He threw his face against it, staring directly into the blinding, white light. It sent him reeling back in momentary blindness.

When he could see again he found another opening in the wall, higher than the first. He jumped up, and got a quick glimpse of an empty room, a giant projector and stacks of film cans. He was dimly aware of voices on the screen, loud, giant voices that filled the theater. Once again he jumped up to look in the projectionist's booth and in the brief moment of one-sided combat with gravity, he again saw the empty room, the machine running smoothly, the hum of it heard dimly through the glass.

But when he landed back on his feet he knew there was no one up there. It was a machine running by itself. It was a picture showing itself. It was like the town and everything in it. Machines, items, things—all unattended. He backed away, banged against the back of the top row of seats and, losing his balance, sprawled head first.

The beam of light kept changing intensity as scenes altered on the screen. There was dialogue and music and it reverberated around the theater. Voices of giants. Music of a million-piece band. And something inside the young man cracked. The small compartment in the back of his mind, where man closets his fears, ties them up, controls and commands them, broke open and they surged across brain and nerves and muscles—a nightmare flood in open rebellion.

The young man scrambled to his feet, sobbing, choking, screaming. He raced down the stairs, through the door, down the steps toward the lobby.

It was when he reached the foot of the steps that he saw the other person. He was directly across the lobby and approaching from a flight of stairs the young man hadn't noticed before. The young man didn't see him clearly nor did he try. He just ran toward him, dimly aware that the other person was running toward him at the same time. In the fraction of a moment that it took him to cross the lobby he had only one thought and that was to reach the other person, to touch him, to hold him. To follow him out to wherever he was going. Out of the building, off the streets, out of the city, because now he knew that he must get away.

It was this thought that filled his mind just before he hit the mirror—a full length mirror that hung on the opposite wall. And he hit it with the force of a hundred and seventy pounds, smashing into it at a dead run. The mirror seemed to explode into a thousand pieces. He found himself on the floor looking at little fragments of his reflection in the small and minute sections of mirror that remained on the wall. It was the picture of a hundred young men lying cut and dazed on the floor of a theater lobby, staring up at what was left of a mirror. And then he lurched to his feet and, like a drunken man in a tilting ship in a heavy sea, he stumbled out of the lobby and out into the street.

Outside it was dark and misty; the streets were wet. The street lights were enveloped in fog and each shone like a dim moon hanging in vapor. He began to run along sidewalks and across streets. He tripped over a bicycle stand and landed on his face, but was on his feet in a moment continuing the mad, headlong, thoughtless, desperate race to no place in particular. He tripped over a curb near the drugstore and again fell on his face, conscious for a moment that he could still feel pain—a jarring, wrenching pain. But only for a moment. He pushed his palms against the sidewalk, forcing himself up and then fell over on his back.

For a moment he lay there, eyes closed. And then he

opened them. A nightmare knocked at his head and asked to come in and ice flowed over his body. He started to scream. An eye was looking at him. A giant eye, bigger than the upper trunk of a man. An unblinking, cold-looking eye was staring at him and his scream never let up, even after he had floundered again to his feet and started to run back toward the park. He was like a human siren disappearing into the dark. Behind him the big painted eye on the optometrist's window stared after him—cold, inhuman and unblinking.

He fell, clutching against a street light. There was a panel with a button which his fingers touched, scrabbled at and finally kept pushing over and over again. A sign over it read, "Push to turn green." He didn't know the sign was there. He only knew he had to push the button and this he kept doing, while the light over the intersection turned red, then yellow, then green, over and over again, responding to the bleeding knuckles of the young man who kept pushing a button and moaning to himself in a soft, barely intelligible chant.

"Please—please, somebody—help me. Help me, somebody. Please. Please. Oh dear God—somebody help me! Won't somebody help me. Won't somebody come—can anyone hear me—?"

The control room was dark and the figures of the uniformed men were silhouetted against the light that came from a small viewing screen on which could be seen the face and upper body of Sergeant Mike Ferris, a youngish looking man in coveralls who kept pushing a button to the right of the screen. Ferris' voice babbled out into the darkness of the control room pleading for help, for someone to listen, for someone to show themselves. It was the sobbing, pleading, supplicating voice of a man whose mind and body were laid bare on a block and the up-and-down intonation seemed naked and embarrassing, as if listened to through a keyhole, with an ear pressed against the door.

The brigadier-general rose, his face strained from long hours of protracted concentration. He was obviously disturbed by the face and voice of the man on the screen. His voice, however, was clipped and authoritative.

"All right, clock him and get him out of there," the general commanded.

A lieutenant-colonel to the general's right reached over, pressed a button and spoke into a panel microphone.

"Release the subject on the double!"

Inside the vast, high ceilinged hangar, men sprang to their feet and ran toward the rectangular metal box that squatted impassively in the center of the huge room. A metal door was swung open. Two non-coms entered followed by an Air Force doctor. Very gently the wires and electrodes were removed from Sergeant Ferris' body. The doctor's hands wandered over his wrists and then propped open his eyes to stare into the dilated pupils. His ear listened to the hollow thumping of an overworked heart. Then Ferris was lifted carefully out and placed on a stretcher.

The medical officer went to the general, where he stood with his staff, staring across the hangar toward the prostrate figure on the stretcher.

The medical officer said, "He's all right, sir. Delusions of some sort, but he's responding all right now."

The general nodded and said, "Can I see him?"

The medical officer nodded and the eight uniformed men walked across the hangar, their feet making a clickety-clack against the concrete as they approached the stretcher. On each of their left shoulders was an insignia patch, indicating that they were members of the Space Technological Research Command, U. S. Air Force. They reached the side of the stretcher and the general leaned over to look closely into the face of Sergeant Mike Ferris.

Ferris' eyes were open now. He turned his face to look up at the general and smiled slightly. The face was wan, pale, bearded. Anguish, loneliness, the misery of some two hundred-odd hours in solitary confinement in a metal box showed in his eyes and the lines of his face.

It was the post-shock look of every wounded man the general had ever seen and while he didn't know Ferris—

that is, didn't know him personally except from sixty typewritten sheets in the man's file that he'd studied intensively before the test, he felt he knew him now. He'd been watching him for over two weeks on the small screen closely, more closely than any human being had been watched before.

The general reminded himself that there should be a medal in this for the sergeant. He had taken what no man had ever taken before. He had remained alone for two hundred and eighty-four hours on a simulated trip to the moon with almost every condition a man might have to face duplicated in the five-by-five box. The wires and electrodes had given a good indication of how the space traveler would react physically. They had charted his respiration, heart action, blood pressure. Beyond this, and most important, they had given a good idea of the point at which a man would break; of the moment a man would succumb to loneliness and try to battle his way out. It was at this moment that Sergeant Mike Ferris had pushed the release button inside his tiny confinement.

The general forced a grin as he leaned over Ferris and said, "How you doing, Sergeant? Feeling better?"

Ferris nodded, "Much better, sir, thank you."

There was a moment's silence before the general spoke again. "Ferris," he asked, "what was it like? Where'd you think you were?"

Ferris stared up toward the high ceiling of the hangar and reflected a moment before he spoke. "A town, sir," he answered. "A town without people . . . without anybody. A place I don't want to go to again." Then he turned to look back toward the general and he said, "What was wrong with me, sir? Just off my rocker or something?"

The general turned toward the medical officer with a nod.

The medical officer said softly, "Just a kind of nightmare your mind manufactured for you, Sergeant. You see, we can feed the stomach with concentrates. We can pump oxygen in and waste materials out. We can supply you with reading for recreation and try to keep your mind occupied."

There was a silence now as the men surrounding the stretcher looked toward the medical officer.

"There's one thing we can't simulate," he continued. "And that's a very basic need. Man's hunger for companionship. That's a barrier we don't know how to breach yet. The barrier of loneliness."

Four aid men lifted Mike Ferris up on the stretcher and carried him across the vast room to the giant doors at the opposite side. He was then carried out into the night where an ambulance had been pulled up and was waiting. Ferris looked up at a giant moon and thought to himself that the next time it would be for real. Not just a box in a hangar. But he was too tired to give it much thought.

They lifted him gently and were about to place him in the rear of the ambulance when Mike Ferris quite accidentally touched his breast pocket. He felt something stiff and took it out of his pocket. The doors of the ambulance shut on him and left him in the quiet darkness of the inside. He heard the engines start and felt the wheels underneath him and was much too tired to reflect on whatever was in his fingers, just a hand's length from his face.

Just a theater ticket—that's all it was. A theater ticket from a small movie house in an empty town. A theater ticket, he thought to himself, and it was in his breast pocket and as the ambulance engines lulled him to sleep and the gently rolling wheels made him close his eyes, he held on to the ticket very tightly. In the morning he'd have to ask himself some questions. In the morning he would have to piece together some impossible fabric of dream and reality. But all that would have to come in the morning. Mike Ferris was much too tired now.

From Rod Serling's closing narration, "Where is Everybody?" The Twilight Zone, October 2, 1959, CBS Television Network.

The CAMERA BEGINS A SLOW PAN back into the room until it is shooting on the box, squatting empty and impassive in the empty room.

NARRATOR'S VOICE
The barrier of loneliness. The palpable,
desperate need of the human animal to
be with his fellow man.

LAP DISSOLVE TO:

NIGHT SKY

The moon and the stars.

NARRATOR'S VOICE
Up there . . . up there in the vastness
of space, in the void that is sky . . .
up there is an enemy known as isolation.
It sits there in the stars waiting . . .
waiting with the patience of eons . . .
forever waiting . . . in The Twilight Zone.

FADE TO BLACK

The Monsters Are Due
On Maple Street

It was Saturday afternoon on Maple Street and the late sun retained some of the warmth of a persistent Indian summer. People along the street marveled at winter's delay and took advantage of it. Lawns were being mowed, cars polished, kids played hopscotch on the sidewalks. Old Mr. Van Horn, the patriarch of the street, who lived alone, had moved his power saw out on his lawn and was fashioning new pickets for his fence. A Good Humor man bicycled in around the corner and was inundated by children and by shouts of "Wait a minute!" from small boys hurrying to con nickels from their parents. It was 4:40 P.M. A football game blared from a portable radio on a front porch, blending with the other sounds of a Saturday afternoon in October. Maple Street. 4:40 P.M. Maple street in its last calm and reflective moments—before the monsters came.

Steve Brand, fortyish, a big man in an old ex-Marine set of dungarees, was washing his car when the lights flashed across the sky. Everyone on the street looked up at the sound of the whoosh and the brilliant flash that dwarfed the sun.

"What was that?" Steve called across at his neighbor, Don Martin, who was fixing a bent spoke on his son's bicycle.

Martin, like everyone else, was cupping his hands over his eyes, to stare up at the sky. He called back to Steve, "Looked like a meteor, didn't it? I didn't hear any crash though, did you?"

Steve shook his head. "Nope. Nothing except that roar."

Steve's wife came out on the front porch. "Steve?" she called. "What was that?"

Steve shut off the water hose. "Guess it was a meteor, honey. Came awful close, didn't it?"

"Much too close for my money," his wife answered. "Much too close."

She went back into the house, and became suddenly conscious of something. All along Maple Street people paused and looked at one another as a gradual awareness took hold. All the sounds had stopped. All of them. There was a silence now. No portable radio. No lawn mowers. No clickety-click of sprinklers that went round and round on front lawns. There was a silence.

Mrs. Sharp, fifty-five years of age, was talking on the telephone, giving a cake recipe to her cousin at the other end of town. Her cousin was asking Mrs. Sharp to repeat the number of eggs when her voice clicked off in the middle of the sentence. Mrs. Sharp, who was not the most patient of women, banged furiously on the telephone hook, screaming for an operator.

Pete Van Horn was right in the middle of sawing a 1 x 4 piece of pine when the power saw went off. He checked the plug, the outlet on the side of the house and then the fuse box in his basement. There was just no power coming in.

Steve Brand's wife, Agnes, came back out on the porch to announce that the oven had stopped working. There was no current or something. Would Steve look at it? Steve couldn't look at it at that moment because he was preoccupied with a hose that suddenly refused to give any more water.

Across the street Charlie Farnsworth, fat and dumpy, in a loud Hawaiian sport shirt that featured hula girls with pineapple baskets on their heads, barged angrily out toward the road, damning any radio outfit that manufactured a portable with the discourtesy to shut off in the middle of a third-quarter forward pass.

Voices built on top of voices until suddenly there was no more silence. There was a conglomeration of questions and protests; of plaintive references to half-cooked dinners, half-watered lawns, half-washed cars, half-finished phone conversations. Did it have anything to do with the meteor? That was the main question—the one most asked. Pete Van Horn disgustedly threw aside the electric cord of his power mower and announced to the group of people who were collected around Steve Brand's station wagon that he was going on over to Bennett Avenue to check and see if the power had gone off there, too. He disappeared into his back yard and was last seen heading into the back yard of the house behind his.

Steve Brand, his face wrinkled with perplexity, leaned against his car door and looked around at the neighbors who had collected. "It just doesn't make sense," he said. "Why should the power go off all of a sudden *and* the phone line?"

Don Martin wiped bicycle grease off his fingers. "Maybe some kind of an electrical storm or something."

Dumpy Charlie's voice was always unpleasantly high. "That just don't seem likely," he squealed. "Sky's just as blue as anything. Not a cloud. No lightning. No thunder. No nothin'. How could it be a storm?"

Mrs. Sharp's face was lined with years, but more deeply by the frustrations of early widowhood. "Well, it's a terrible thing when a phone company can't keep its line open," she complained. "Just a terrible thing."

"What about my portable radio," Charlie demanded. "Ohio State's got the ball on Southern Methodist's eighteen-yard line. They throw a pass and the damn thing goes off just then."

There was a murmur in the group as people looked at one another and heads were shaken.

Charlie picked his teeth with a dirty thumb nail. "Steve," he said in his high, little voice, "why don't you go downtown and check with the police?"

"They'll probably think we're crazy or something," Don Martin said. "A little power failure and right away we get all flustered and everything."

"It isn't just the power failure," Steve answered. "If if was, we'd still be able to get a broadcast on the portable."

There was a murmur of reaction to this and heads nodded.

Steve opened the door to his station wagon. "I'll run downtown. We'll get this all straightened out."

He inched his big frame onto the front seat behind the wheel, turned on the ignition and pushed the starter button. There was no sound. The engine didn't even turn over. He tried it a couple of times more, and still there was no response. The others stared silently at him. He scratched his jaw.

"Doesn't that beat all? It was working fine before."

"Out of gas?" Don offered.

Steve shook his head. "I just had it filled up."

"What's it mean?" Mrs. Sharp asked.

Charlie Farnsworth's piggish little eyes flapped open and shut. "It's just as if—just as if everything had stopped. You better *walk* downtown, Steve."

"I'll go with you," Don said.

Steve got out of the car, shut the door and turned to Don. "Couldn't be a meteor," he said. "A meteor couldn't do *this*." He looked off in thought for a moment, then nodded. "Come on, let's go."

They started to walk away from the group, when they heard the boy's voice. Tommy Bishop, aged twelve, had stepped out in front of the others and was calling out to them.

"Mr. Brand! Mr. Martin. You better not leave!"

Steve took a step back toward him.

"Why not?" he asked.

"They don't want you to," Tommy said.

Steve and Don exchanged a look.

"*Who* doesn't want us to?" Steve asked him.

Tommy looked up toward the sky. "Them," he said.

"Them?" Steve asked.

"Who are 'them'?" Charlie squealed.

"Whoever was in that thing that came by overhead," Tommy said intently.

Steve walked slowly back toward the boy and stopped close to him. "What, Tommy?" he asked.

"Whoever was in that thing that came over," Tommy repeated. "I don't think they want us to leave here."

Steve knelt down in front of the boy "What do you mean, Tommy? What are you talking about?"

"They don't want us to leave, that's why they shut everything off."

"What makes you say that?" Irritation crept into Steve's voice. "Whatever gave you *that* idea?"

Mrs. Sharp pushed her way through to the front of the crowd. "That's the craziest thing I ever heard," she announced in a public-address-system voice. "Just about the craziest thing I ever did hear!"

Tommy could feel the unwillingness to believe him. "It's always that way," he said defensively, "in every story I've ever read about a space ship landing from outer space!"

Charlie Farnsworth whinnied out his derision.

Mrs. Sharp waggled a bony finger in front of Tommy's mother. "If you ask me, Sally Bishop," she said, "you'd better get that boy of yours up to bed. He's been reading too many comic books or seeing too many movies or something."

Sally Bishop's face reddened. She gripped Tommy's shoulders tightly. "Tommy," she said softly. "Stop that kind of talk, honey."

Steve's eyes never left the boy's face. "That's all right, Tom. We'll be right back. You'll see. That wasn't a ship or anything like it. That was just a—a meteor or something, likely as not—" He turned to the group, trying to weight his words with an optimism he didn't quite feel. "No doubt it did have something to do with all this power failure and the rest of it. Meteors can do crazy things. Like sun spots."

"That's right," Don said, as if picking up a cue. "Like sun spots. That kind of thing. They can raise cain with radio reception all over the world. And this thing being so close—why there's no telling what sort of stuff it can do." He wet his lips nervously. "Come on, Steve. We'll go into town and see if that isn't what's causing it all."

Once again the two men started away.

"Mr. Brand!" Tommy's voice was defiant and frightened at the same time. He pulled away from his mother and ran after them. "Please, Mr. Brand, please don't leave here."

There was a stir, a rustle, a movement among the people. There was something about the boy. Something about the intense little face. Something about the words that carried such emphasis, such belief, such fear. They listened to these words and rejected them because intellect and logic had no room for spaceships and greenheaded things. But the irritation that showed in the eyes, the murmuring and the compressed lips had nothing to do with intellect. A little boy was bringing up fears that shouldn't be brought up; and the people on Maple Street this Saturday afternoon were no different from any other set of human beings. Order, reason, logic were slipping, pushed by the wild conjectures of a twelve-year-old boy.

"Somebody ought to spank that kid," an angry voice muttered.

Tommy Bishop's voice continued defiant. It pierced the murmurings and rose above them. "You might not even be able to get to town," he said. "It was that way in the story. *Nobody* could leave. Nobody except—"

"Except who?" Steve asked.

"Except the people they'd sent down ahead of them. They looked just like humans. It wasn't until the ship landed that—"

His mother grabbed him by the arm and pulled him back. "Tommy," she said in a low voice. "Please, honey . . . don't talk that way."

"Damn right he shouldn't talk that way," came the voice of the man in the rear again. "And we shouldn't stand here listening to him. Why this is the craziest thing I ever heard. The kid tells us a comic-book plot and here we stand listening—"

His voice died away as Steve stood up and faced the crowd. Fear can throw people into a panic, but it can also make them receptive to a leader and Steve Brand at this moment was such a leader. The big man in the ex-Marine dungarees had an authority about him.

"Go ahead, Tommy," he said to the boy. "What kind of story was this? What about the people that they sent out ahead?"

"That was the way they prepared things for the landing, Mr. Brand," Tommy said. "They sent four people. A mother and a father and two kids who looked just like humans. But they weren't."

There was a murmur—a stir of uneasy laughter. People looked at one another again and a couple of them smiled.

"Well," Steve said, lightly but carefully, "I guess we'd better run a check on the neighborhood, and see which ones of us are really human."

His words were a release. Laughter broke out openly. But soon it died away. Only Charlie Farnsworth's horse whinny persisted over the growing silence and then he too lapsed into a grim quietness, until all fifteen people were looking at one another through changed eyes. A twelve-year-old boy had planted a seed. And something was growing out of the street with invisible branches that began to wrap themselves around the men and women and pull them apart. Distrust lay heavy in the air.

Suddenly there was the sound of a car engine and all heads turned as one. Across the street Ned Rosen was sitting in his convertible trying to start it, and nothing was happening beyond the labored sound of a sick engine getting deeper and hoarser and finally giving up altogether. Ned Rosen, a thin, serious-faced man in his thirties, got out of his car and closed the door. He stood there staring at it for a moment, shook his head, looked across the street at his neighbors and started toward them.

"Can't get her started, Ned?" Don Martin called out to him.

"No dice," Ned answered. "Funny, she was working fine this morning."

Without warning, all by itself, the car started up and idled smoothly, smoke briefly coming out of the exhaust.

Ned Rosen whirled around to stare at it, his eyes wide. Then, just as suddenly as it started, the engine sputtered and stopped.

"Started all by itself!" Charlie Farnsworth squealed excitedly.

"How did it do that?" Mrs. Sharp asked. "How could it just start all by itself?"

Sally Bishop let loose her son's arm and just stood there, shaking her head. "How in the world—" she began.

Then there were no more questions. They stood silently staring at Ned Rosen who looked from them to his car and then back again. He went to the car and looked at it. Then he scratched his head again.

"Somebody explain it to me," he said. "I sure never saw anything like that happen before!"

"He never did come out to look at that thing that flew overhead. He wasn't even interested." Don Martin said heavily.

"What do you say we ask him some questions," Charlie Farnsworth proposed importantly. "I'd like to know what's going on here!"

There was a chorus of assent and the fifteen people started across the street toward Ned Rosen's driveway. Unity was restored, they had a purpose, a feeling of activity and direction. They were *doing* something. They weren't sure what, but Ned Rosen was flesh and blood—askable, reachable and seeable. He watched with growing apprehension as his neighbors marched toward him. They stopped on the sidewalk close to the driveway and surveyed him.

Ned Rosen pointed to his car. "I just don't understand it, any more than you do! I tried to start it and it *wouldn't* start. You saw me. All of you saw me."

His neighbors seemed massed against him, solidly, alarmingly.

"I don't understand it!" he cried. "I swear—I don't understand. What's happening?"

Charlie Farnsworth stood out in front of the others. "Maybe you better tell us," he demanded. "Nothing's working on this street. Nothing. No lights, no power, no radio. Nothing except one car—*yours*!"

There were mutterings from the crowd. Steve Brand stood back by himself and said nothing. He didn't like what was going on. Something was building up that threatened to grow beyond control.

"Come on, Rosen," Charlie Farnsworth commanded shrilly, "let's hear what goes on! Let's hear how you explain your car startin' like that!"

Ned Rosen wasn't a coward. He was a quiet man who didn't like violence and had never been a physical fighter. But he didn't like being bullied. Ned Rosen got mad.

"Hold it!" he shouted. "Just hold it. You keep your distance. All of you. All right, I've got a car that starts by itself. Well, that's a freak thing—I admit it! But does that make me some sort of a criminal or something? I don't know why the car works—it just does!"

The crowd were neither sobered nor reassured by Rosen's words, but they were not too frightened to listen. They huddled together, mumbling, and Ned Rosen's eyes went from face to face till they stopped on Steve Brand's. Ned knew Steve Brand. Of all the men on the street, this seemed the guy with the most substance. The most intelligent. The most essentially decent.

"What's it all about, Steve?" he asked.

"We're all on a monster kick, Ned," he answered quietly. "Seems that the general impression holds that maybe one family isn't what we think they are. Monsters from outer space or something. Different from us. Fifth columnists from the vast beyond." He couldn't keep the sarcasm out of his voice. "Do you know anybody around here who might fit that description?"

Rosen's eyes narrowed. "What is this, a gag?" He looked around the group again. "This a practical joke or something?" And without apparent reason, without logic, without explanation, his car started again, idled for a moment, sending smoke out of the exhaust, and stopped.

A woman began to cry, and the bank of eyes facing Ned Rosen looked cold and accusing. He walked to his porch steps and stood on them, facing his neighbors.

"Is that supposed to incriminate me?" he asked. "The car engine goes on and off and that really does it, huh?"

He looked down into their faces. "I don't understand it. Not any more than you do."

He could tell that they were unmoved. This couldn't really be happening, Ned thought to himself.

"Look," he said in a different tone. "You all know me. We've lived here four years. Right in this house. We're no different from any of the rest of you!" He held out his hands toward them. The people he was looking at hardly resembled the people he'd lived alongside of for the past four years. They looked as if someone had taken a brush and altered every character with a few strokes. "Really," he continued, "this whole thing is just . . . just weird—"

"Well, if that's the case, Ned Rosen," Mrs. Sharp's voice suddenly erupted from the crowd—"maybe you'd better explain why—" She stopped abruptly and clamped her mouth shut, but looked wise and pleased with herself.

"Explain what?" Rosen asked her softly.

Steve Brand sensed a special danger now. "Look," he said, "let's forget this right now—"

Charlie Farnsworth cut him off. "Go ahead. Let her talk. What about it? Explain what?"

Mrs. Sharp, with an air of great reluctance, said, "Well, sometimes I go to bed late at night. A couple of times— a couple of times I've come out on the porch, and I've seen Ned Rosen here, in the wee hours of the morning, standing out in front of his house looking up at the sky." She looked around the circle of faces. "That's right, looking up at the sky as if—as if he was waiting for something." She paused for emphasis, for dramatic effect. "As if he was looking for something!" she repeated.

The nail on the coffin, Steve Brand thought. One, dumb, ordinary, simple idiosyncrasy of a human being— and that probably was all it would take. He heard the murmuring of the crowd rise and saw Ned Rosen's face turn white. Rosen's wife, Ann, came out on the porch. She took a look at the crowd and then at her husband's face.

"What's going on, Ned?" she asked.

"I don't know what's going on," Ned answered. "I just don't know, Ann. But I'll tell you this. I don't like these people. I don't like what they're doing. I don't like them standing in my yard like this. And if any one of them takes another step and gets close to my porch—I'll break his jaw. I swear to God, that's just what I'll do. I'll break his jaw. Now go on, get out of here, all of you!" he shouted at them. "Get the hell out of here."

"Ned," Ann's voice was shocked.

"You heard me," Ned repeated. "All of you get out of here."

None of them eager to start an action, the people began to back away. But they had an obscure sense of gratification. At least there was an opponent now. Someone who wasn't one of them. And this gave them a kind of secure feeling. The enemy was no longer formless and vague. The enemy had a front porch and a front yard and a car. And he had shouted threats at them.

They started slowly back across the street forgetting for the moment what had started it all. Forgetting that there was no power, and no telephones. Forgetting even that there had been a meteor overhead not twenty minutes earlier. It wasn't until much later, as a matter of fact, that anyone posed a certain question.

Old man Van Horn had walked through his back yard over to Bennett Avenue. He'd never come back. Where was he? It was not one of the questions that passed through the minds of any of the thirty or forty people on Maple Street who sat on their front porches and watched the night come and felt the now menacing darkness close in on them.

There were lanterns lit all along Maple Street by ten o'clock. Candles shone through living-room windows and cast flickering, unsteady shadows all along the street. Groups of people huddled on front lawns around their lanterns and a soft murmur of voices was carried over the Indian-summer night air. All eyes eventually were drawn to Ned Rosen's front porch.

He sat there on the railing, observing the little points of light spotted around in the darkness. He knew he was surrounded. He was the animal at bay.

His wife came out on the porch and brought him a

glass of lemonade. Her face was white and strained. Like her husband, Ann Rosen was a gentle person, unarmored by temper or any proclivity for outrage. She stood close to her husband now on the darkened porch feeling the suspicion that flowed from the people around lanterns, thinking to herself that these were people she had entertained in her house. These were women she talked to over clotheslines in the back yard; people who had been friends and neighbors only that morning. Oh dear God, could all this have happened in those few hours? It must be a nightmare, she thought. It had to be a nightmare that she could wake up from. It couldn't be anything else.

Across the street Mabel Farnsworth, Charlie's wife, shook her head and clucked at her husband who was drinking a can of beer. "It just doesn't seem right though, Charlie, keeping watch on them. Why he was right when he said he was one of our neighbors. I've known Ann Rosen ever since they moved in. We've been good friends."

Charlie Farnsworth turned to her disgustedly. "That don't prove a thing," he said. "Any guy who'd spend his time lookin' up at the sky early in the morning—well there's something wrong with that kind of person. There's something that ain't legitimate. Maybe under normal circumstances we could let it go by. But these aren't normal circumstances." He turned and pointed toward the street. "Look at that," he said. "Nothin' but candles and lanterns. Why it's like goin' back into the Dark Ages or something!"

He was right. Maple Street had changed with the night. The flickering lights had done something to its character. It looked odd and menacing and very different. Up and down the street, people noticed it. The change in Maple Street. It was the feeling one got after being away from home for many, many years and then returning. There was a vague familiarity about it, but it wasn't the same. It was different.

Ned Rosen and his wife heard footsteps coming toward their house. Ned got up from the railing and shouted out into the darkness.

"Whoever it is, just stay right where you are. I don't want any trouble, but if anybody sets foot on my porch, that's what they're going to get—trouble!" He saw that it was Steve Brand and his features relaxed.

"Ned," Steve began.

Ned Rosen cut him off. "I've already explained to you people, I don't sleep very well at night sometimes. I get up and I take a walk and I look up at the sky. I look at the stars."

Ann Rosen's voice shook as she stood alongside of him. "That's exactly what he does. Why this whole thing, it's—it's some kind of a madness or something."

Steve Brand stood on the sidewalk and nodded grimly. "That's exactly what it is—some kind of madness."

Charlie Farnsworth's voice from the adjoining yard was spiteful. "You'd best watch who you're seen with, Steve. Until we get this all straightened out, you ain't exactly above suspicion yourself."

Steve whirled around to the outline of the fat figure that stood behind the lantern in the other yard. "Or you either, Charlie," he shouted. "Or any of the rest of us!"

Mrs. Sharp's voice came from the darkness across the street. "What I'd like to know is—what are we going to do? Just stand around here all night?"

"There's nothin' else we can do," Charlie Farnsworth said. He looked wisely over toward Ned Rosen's house. "One of 'em'll tip their hand. They *got* to."

It was Charlie's voice that did it for Steve Brand at this moment. The shrieking, pig squeal that came from the layers of fat and the idiotic sport shirt and the dull, dumb, blind prejudice of the man. "There's something *you* can do, Charlie," Steve called out to him. "You can go inside your house and keep your mouth shut!"

"You sound real anxious to have that happen, Steve," Charlie's voice answered him back from the little spot of light in the next yard. "I think we'd better keep our eye on you, too!"

Don Martin came up to Steve Brand, carrying a lantern. There was something hesitant in his manner, as if he were about to take a bit in his teeth, but wondered whether it would hurt. "I think everything might as well come out now," Don said. "I really do. I think everything should come out."

People came off porches, from front yards, to stand around in a group near Don who now turned directly toward Steve.

"Your wife's done plenty of talking, Steve, about how odd you are," he said.

Charlie Farnsworth trotted over. "Go ahead. Tell us what she said," he demanded excitedly.

Steve Brand knew this was the way it would happen. He was not really surprised but he still felt a hot anger rise up inside of him. "Go ahead," he said. "What's my wife said? Let's get it *all* out." He peered around at the shadowy figures of the neighbors. "Let's pick out every Goddamned peculiarity of every single man, woman and child on this street! Don't stop with me and Ned. How about a firing squad at dawn, so we can get rid of all the suspects! Make it easier for you!"

Don Martin's voice retreated fretfully. "There's no need getting so upset, Steve—"

"Go to hell, Don," Steve said to him in a cold and dispassionate fury.

Needled, Don went on the offensive again but his tone held something plaintive and petulant. "It just so happens that, well, Agnes has talked about how there's plenty of nights you've spent hours in your basement working on some kind of a radio or something. Well none of us have ever *seen* that radio—"

"Go ahead, Steve," Charlie Farnsworth yelled at him. "What kind of a 'radio set' you workin' on? I never seen it. Neither has anyone else. Who do you talk to on that radio set? And who talks to you?"

Steve's eyes slowly traveled in an arc over the hidden faces and the shrouded forms of neighbors who were now accusers. "I'm surprised at you, Charlie," he said quietly. "I really am. How come you're so God-damned dense all of a sudden? Who do I talk to? I talk to monsters from outer space. I talk to three-headed green men who fly over here in what look like meteors!"

Agnes Brand walked across the street to stand at her

husband's elbow. She pulled at his arm with frightened intensity. "Steve! Steve, please," she said. "It's just a ham radio set," she tried to explain. "That's all. I bought him a book on it myself. It's just a ham radio set. A lot of people have them. I can show it to you. It's right down in the basement."

Steve pulled her hand off his arm. "You show them nothing," he said to her. "If they want to look inside our house, let them get a search warrant!"

Charlie's voice whined at him. "Look, buddy, you can't afford to—"

"Charlie," Steve shouted at him. "Don't tell me what I can afford. And stop telling me who's dangerous and who isn't. And who's safe and who's a menace!" He walked over to the edge of the road and saw that people backed away from him. "And you're with him—all of you," Steve bellowed at them. "You're standing there all set to crucify—to find a scapegoat—desperate to point some kind of a finger at a neighbor!" There was intensity in his tone and on his face, accentuated by the flickering light of the lanterns and the candles. "Well look, friends, the only thing that's going to happen is that we'll eat each other up alive. Understand? *We are going to eat each other up alive!*"

Charlie Farnsworth suddenly ran over to him and grabbed his arm. "That's not the *only* thing that can happen to us," he said in a frightened, hushed voice. "Look!"

"Oh, my God," Don Martin said.

Mrs. Sharp screamed. All eyes turned to look down the street where a figure had suddenly materialized in the darkness and the sound of measured footsteps on concrete grew louder and louder as it walked toward them. Sally Bishop let out a stifled cry and grabbed Tommy's shoulder.

The child's voice screamed out, "It's the monster! It's the monster!"

There was a frightened wail from another woman, and the residents of Maple Street stood transfixed with terror as something unknown came slowly down the street. Don Martin disappeared and came back out of his house a moment later carrying a shotgun. He pointed it toward the approaching form. Steve pulled it out of his hands.

"For God's sake, will somebody think a thought around here? Will you people wise up? What good would a shotgun do against—"

A quaking, frightened Charlie Farnsworth grabbed the gun from Steve's hand. "No more talk, Steve," he said. "You're going to talk us into a grave! You'd let whoever's out there walk right over us, wouldn't yuh? Well, some of us won't!"

He swung the gun up and pulled the trigger. The noise was a shocking, shattering intrusion and it echoed and re-echoed through the night. A hundred yards away the figure collapsed like a piece of clothing blown off a line by the wind. From front porches and lawns people raced toward it.

Steve was the first to reach him. He knelt down, turned him over and looked at his face. Then he looked up toward the semi-circle of silent faces surveying him.

"All right, friends," he said quietly. "It happened. We got our first victim—Pete Van Horn!"

"Oh, my God," Don Martin said in a hushed voice. "He was just going over to the next block to see if the power was on—"

Mrs. Sharp's voice was that of injured justice. "You killed him, Charlie! You shot him dead!"

Charlie Farnsworth's face looked like a piece of uncooked dough, quivering and shaking in the light of the lantern he held.

"I didn't know who he was," he said. "I certainly didn't know who he was." Tears rolled down his fat cheeks. "He comes walking out of the dark—how am I supposed to know who he was?" He looked wildly around and then grabbed Steve's arm. Steve could explain things to people. "Steve," he screamed, "you know why I shot. How was I supposed to know he wasn't a monster or something?"

Steve looked at him and didn't say anything. Charlie grabbed Don.

"We're all scared of the same thing," he blubbered. "The very same thing. I was just tryin' to protect my home, that's all. Look, all of you, that's all I was tryin' to do!" He tried to shut out the sight of Pete Van Horn who stared up at him with dead eyes and a shattered chest. "Please, please, please," Charlie Farnsworth sobbed, "I didn't know it was somebody we knew. I swear to God I didn't know—"

The lights went on in Charlie Farnsworth's house and shone brightly on the people of Maple Street. They looked suddenly naked. They blinked foolishly at the lights and their mouths gaped like fishes'.

"Charlie," Mrs. Sharp said, like a judge pronouncing sentence, "how come you're the only one with lights on now?"

Ned Rosen nodded in agreement. "That's what I'd like to know," he said. Something inside tried to check him, but his anger made him go on. "How come, Charlie? You're quiet all of a sudden. You've got nothing to say out of that big, fat mouth of yours. Well, let's hear it, Charlie? Let's hear why you've got lights!"

Again the chorus of voices that punctuated the request and gave it legitimacy and a vote of support. "Why, Charlie?" the voices asked him. "How come you're the only one with lights?" The questions came out of the night to land against his fat wet cheeks. "You were so quick to kill," Ned Rosen continued, "and you were so quick to tell us who we had to be careful of. Well maybe you *had* to kill, Charlie. Maybe Pete Van Horn, God rest his soul, was trying to tell us something. Maybe he'd found out something and had come back to tell us who there was among us we should watch out for."

Charlie's eyes were little pits of growing fear as he backed away from the people and found himself up against a bush in front of his house. "No," he said. "No, please." His chubby hands tried to speak for him. They waved around, pleading. The palms outstretched, begging for forgiveness and understanding. "Please—please, I swear to you—it isn't me! It really isn't me."

A stone hit him on the side of the face and drew blood. He screamed and clutched at his face as the people began to converge on him.

"No," he screamed. "No."

Like a hippopotamus in a circus, he scrambled over

the bush, tearing his clothes and scratching his face and arms. His wife tried to run toward him, somebody stuck a foot out and she tripped, sprawling head first on the sidewalk. Another stone whistled through the air and hit Charlie on the back of the head as he raced across his front yard toward his porch. A rock smashed at the porch light and sent glass cascading down on his head.

"It isn't me," he screamed back at them as they came toward him across the front lawn. "It isn't me, but I know who it is," he said suddenly, without thought. Even as he said it, he realized it was the only possible thing to say.

People stopped, motionless as statues, and a voice called out from the darkness. "All right, Charlie, who is it?"

He was a grotesque, fat figure of a man who smiled now through the tears and the blood that cascaded down his face. "Well, I'm going to tell you," he said. "I am now going to tell you, because I know who it is. I really know who it is. It's . . ."

"Go ahead, Charlie," a voice commanded him. "Who's the monster?"

Don Martin pushed his way to the front of the crowd. "All right, Charlie, now! Let's hear it!"

Charlie tried to think. He tried to come up with a name. A nightmare engulfed him. Fear whipped at the back of his brain. "It's the kid," he screamed. "That's who it is. It's the kid!"

Sally Bishop screamed and grabbed at Tommy, burying his face against her. "That's crazy," she said to the people who now stared at her. "That's crazy. He's a little boy."

"But he knew," said Mrs. Sharp. "He was the only one who knew. He told us all about it. Well how did he know? How *could* he have known?"

Voices supported her. "How could he know?" "Who told him?" "Make the kid answer." A fever had taken hold now, a hot, burning virus that twisted faces and forced out words and solidified the terror inside of each person on Maple Street.

Tommy broke away from his mother and started to

run. A man dove at him in a flying tackle and missed. Another man threw a stone wildly toward the darkness. They began to run after him down the street. Voices shouted through the night, women screamed. A small child's voice protested—a playmate of Tommy's, one tiny voice of sanity in the middle of a madness as men and women ran down the street, the sidewalks, the curbs, looking blindly for a twelve-year-old boy.

And then suddenly the lights went on in another house —a two-story, gray stucco house that belonged to Bob Weaver. A man screamed, "It isn't the kid. It's Bob Weaver's house!"

A porch light went on at Mrs. Sharp's house and Sally Bishop screamed, "It isn't Bob Weaver's house. It's Mrs. Sharp's place."

"I tell you it's the kid," Charlie screamed.

The lights went on and off, on and off down the street. A power mower suddenly began to move all by itself lurching crazily across a front yard, cutting an irregular path of grass until it smashed against the side of the house.

"It's Charlie," Don Martin screamed. "He's the one." And then he saw his own lights go on and off.

They ran this way and that way, over to one house and then back across the street to another. A rock flew through the air and then another. A pane of glass smashed and there was the cry of a woman in pain. Lights on and off, on and off. Charlie Farnsworth went down on his knees as a piece of brick plowed a two-inch hole in the back of his skull. Mrs. Sharp lay on her back screaming, and felt the tearing jab of a woman's high heel in her mouth as someone stepped on her, racing across the street.

From a quarter of a mile away, on a hilltop, Maple Street looked like this, a long tree-lined avenue full of lights going on and off and screaming people racing back and forth. Maple Street was a bedlam. It was an outdoor asylum for the insane. Windows were broken, street lights sent clusters of broken glass down on the heads of women and children. Power mowers started up and car engines and radios. Blaring music mixed with the screams and shouts and the anger.

Up on top of the hill two men, screened by the darkness, stood near the entrance to a space ship and looked down on Maple Street.

"Understand the procedure now?" the first figure said. "Just stop a few of their machines and radios and telephones and lawn mowers. Throw them into darkness for a few hours and then watch the pattern unfold."

"And this pattern is always the same?" the second figure asked.

"With few variations," came the answer. "They pick the most dangerous enemy they can find and it's themselves. All we need do is sit back—and watch."

"Then I take it," figure two said, "this place, this Maple Street, is not unique?"

Figure one shook his head and laughed. "By no means. Their world is full of Maple Streets and we'll go from one to the other and let them destroy themselves." He started up the incline toward the entrance of the space ship. "One to the other," he said as the other figure followed him. "One to the other." There was just the echo of his voice as the two figures disappeared and a panel slid softly across the entrance. "One to the other," the echo said.

When the sun came up on the following morning Maple Street was silent. Most of the houses had been burned. There were a few bodies lying on sidewalks and draped over porch railings. But the silence was total. There simply was no more life. At four o'clock that afternoon there was no more world, or at least not the kind of world that had greeted the morning. And by Wednesday afternoon of the following week, a new set of residents had moved into Maple Street. They were a handsome race of people. Their faces showed great character. Great character indeed. Great character and excellently shaped heads. Excellently shaped heads—two to each new resident!

From Rod Serling's closing narration, "The Monsters Are

Due on Maple Street," The Twilight Zone, January 1, 1960, CBS Television Network.

Now the CAMERA PANS UP for a shot of the starry sky and over this we hear the Narrator's Voice.

> NARRATOR'S VOICE
> The tools of conquest do not necessarily
> come with bombs and explosions and
> fall-out. There are weapons that
> are simply thoughts, attitudes, preju-
> dices—to be found only in the minds
> of men. For the record, prejudices can
> kill and suspicion can destroy and a
> thoughtless, frightened search for a
> scapegoat has a fall-out all of its own
> for the children . . . and the children yet
> unborn.
> (a pause)
> And the pity of it is, that these
> things cannot be confined to . . . The
> Twilight Zone!
>
> FADE TO BLACK

OUT OF THIS WORLD!

That's the only way to describe Bantam's great series of science-fiction classics. These space-age thrillers are filled with terror, fancy and adventure and written by America's most renowned writers of science fiction. Welcome to outer space and have a good trip!

☐	FANTASTIC VOYAGE by Isaac Asimov	2477	$1.25
☐	STAR TREK: THE NEW VOYAGES by Culbreath & Marshak	2719	$1.75
☐	THE MYSTERIOUS ISLAND by Jules Verne	2872	$1.25
☐	ALAS, BABYLON by Pat Frank	2923	$1.75
☐	A CANTICLE FOR LEBOWITZ by Walter Miller, Jr.	2973	$1.75
☐	RAGA SIX by Frank Lauria	7249	$1.25
☐	THE MARTIAN CHRONICLES by Ray Bradbury	7900	$1.25
☐	HELLSTROM'S HIVE by Frank Herbert	8276	$1.50
☐	HIERO'S JOURNEY by Sterling Lanier	8534	$1.25
☐	DHALGREN by Samuel R. Delany	8554	$1.95
☐	STAR TREK XI by James Blish	8717	$1.75
☐	THE DAY OF THE DRONES by A. M. Lightner	10057	$1.25
☐	THE TOMBS OF ATUAN by Ursula LeGuin	10132	$1.75
☐	20,000 LEAGUES UNDER THE SEA by Jules Verne	10325	$1.25

Buy them at your local bookstore or use this handy coupon for ordering:

THE TWILIGHT ZONE

Rod Serling, one of America's exciting writers, has fashioned amazing excursions into the fifth dimension—the world of imagination. Here are six brilliant collections of fantastic stories written expressly for Bantam. Discover, for yourself, the fascinating world of Rod Serling in:

Hair-raising happenings
that guarantee nightmares!

You'll be fascinated by unearthly events, intrigued by stories of weird and bizarre occurrences, startled by terrifying tales that border fact and fiction, truth and fantasy. Look for these titles or use the handy coupon below. Go beyond time and space into the strange mysteries of all times!

☐	TIMELESS STORIES FOR TODAY AND TOMORROW by Ray Bradbury, ed.	10249 •	$1.50
☐	STRANGER THAN SCIENCE by Frank Edwards	8043 •	95¢
☐	GREAT TALES OF HORROR by Edgar Allan Poe	7935 •	$1.25
☐	THIS BAFFLING WORLD III by John Godwin	7758 •	95¢
☐	50 TRUE TALES OF TERROR by John Canning, ed.	7755 •	$1.50
☐	50 GREAT GHOST STORIES by John Canning, ed.	6927 •	$1.50
☐	50 GREAT HORROR STORIES by John Canning, ed.	2851 •	$1.95
☐	DEVILS AND DEMONS by Rod Serling, ed.	2850 •	$1.25
☐	THE TIME MACHINE by H. G. Wells	2783 •	95¢
☐	THIS BAFFLING WORLD by John Godwin	2706 •	$1.25
☐	SEVEN MASTERPIECES OF GOTHIC HORROR by Robert Donald Spector, ed.	2465 •	$1.50

Buy them at your local bookstore or use this handy coupon for ordering: